LIBERTY SQUARE

A Kate Delafield Mystery

Katherine V. FORREST

Spinsters Ink
2008

Spinsters Ink
P.O. Box 242
Midway, Florida 32343

Printing History:
Berkley Prime Crime hardcover edition - September, 1996
Berkley Prime Crime mass-market edition - July, 1997
Berkley Prime Crime trade paperback edition - November, 2000

Spinsters Ink First Edition - March, 2008

Cover designer: Linda Callaghan

ISBN-10: 1-883523-66-4
ISBN-10: 978-1-883523-66-4

For Jo

Acknowledgments

To "Louise," of the United States Marine Corps, for technical detail surrounding Kate Delafield's time in the Corps and in Vietnam. It is this nation's shame that I cannot reveal the true identity of an American citizen who has dedicated twenty years of her life in service to her country.

To Jo Hercus, partner in crime and partner in life, for creative survival techniques and emotional nourishment.

To Montserrat Fontes, brilliant novelist and great friend, whose passionate advocacy for Aimee and the wholeness of Kate helped fuel this novel.

To Cath Walker for vital feedback when it really, really mattered.

To Diane Bennison of Madwoman Press, Northboro, MA, for leading me to "Louise."

To my writer-brother Michael Nava.

To the inestimable Richard LaBonte.

To Mitch Grobeson for what he's done for us all.

To Natalee Rosenstein for very fine editorial suggestions.

To Charlotte Sheedy for bringing it all together.

1

KATE Delafield waited impatiently at the intersection of Pennsylvania Avenue and 9th Street, searching rush hour traffic for a maroon Chevy Cavalier. She glanced at her watch: 5:15. Fifteen minutes later than when she said she would be here, and Aimee would not be annoyed in the least—which served only to increase Kate's own irritation.

She wished she could signal any of the taxi drivers eyeing her from passing vehicles, wished she had not insisted on a rental car. She wanted the Chevy Cavalier here right now, wanted the armor of a car around her. She felt exposed, uneasy, and off balance in Washington, D.C., on this November day in 1994. Images, branded into her from the picture books of childhood and sketchy recollections of visits during her decades-ago training at the Marine Corps base nearby, clashed against the unsettling changes to this place; a chaos of strange new patches had been added to a familiar old quilt of a city.

Across the street stood the granite Grecian columns of the Justice Department Building; a short distance away on either side of her the two most sanctified features of this city, the White House and the dominating

Capitol dome. But behind her was the lego-block FBI Building from which she had just emerged—one of the quilt's new patches. As was the subject matter of the seminar she had attended: behavioral profiles of the psychopaths infesting the cities of America. In this very city the "normal" murder rate had overwhelmed the capabilities of its Metropolitan Police Force. And although any large city contained its dangers, at least the dangers in the streets of her own city, Los Angeles, were those she knew.

The breeze had edged to crispness after the day's earlier showers, scudding a few stray gold leaves along the curb. Kate hunched her shoulders inside her raincoat, her gaze drawn briefly to a maple tree with only vestiges remaining of its fall splendor, like a withered old lady with rouge spots on her cheeks. She thought of the Michigan autumns of her youth, the blazing golds and reds of maple, oak, elm, grudgingly falling away to expose branches of icy brittle lace against the gray clouds of winter, against sere, fallow fields, frost-covered red barns. . . . Her gaze rose to clouds gathering to obscure a milky sky. Where *was* Aimee?

A police car drifted past, and Kate took in its occupants, an African-American female and a white male, then she studied the car itself: white, with a red, white, and blue light bar on its roof, a wide aquamarine swath along the side, a gold shield adorning the door. For her, the presence of the patrol car in a city bristling with police presence safeguarding some of the most prestigious officeholders in the world conferred neither security nor protection—nor did standing in front of the building housing the foremost police organization in the world. Washington, D.C., was falling apart, its civil services in a state of budgetary mismanagement and near-collapse, and everyone knew it. For all its massive buildings and marble monuments, this majestic city felt as dangerous to her as the deadliest alleys of Los Angeles.

Finally, out of the next flotilla of cars released by a stoplight on the wide boulevard, the maroon Chevy Cavalier swung over to the curb.

"Hope you didn't have to drive around too much," Kate said, tossing her shoulder bag and briefcase into the backseat, wrestling the seat belt into place. She brushed a hand over Aimee's thigh, resting it there. "Sorry I'm late. I like the sweatshirt," she said. The color was odd—burnt orange—and she could not quite make out its sports logo, but it hung attractively on Aimee's slender shoulders, its sleeves pushed up to her elbows. "Have fun today?"

Aimee flashed her a quick grin, squeezed Kate's hand on her thigh. "We went to the Space Museum. I need two more weeks here at least!" A practiced head shake flung a lock of dark hair away from Aimee's eyes. "Anything would be better than spending a day in a place named for the asshole of the century."

"High-Heels Hoover," Kate said, quoting her pal Joe D'Amico's scathing mockery of J. Edgar Hoover's supposedly hidden life. "Little did we know."

"His building looks just like him—squat, ugly, sinister."

Kate murmured assent. Penetrating the FBI Building's high-tech security had required scanning and registration, a laminated ID tag, entry through a turnstile and past a processing slot for the ID tag—all of which granted monitored access to a warren of dauntingly anonymous corridors.

Aimee's hands tightened on the steering wheel. "The man poisoned so many lives . . ."

Kate nodded. Nothing needed to be said. She and Aimee had met during the course of an investigation that had proven the ongoing pervasiveness of that poison.

Aimee asked, "So what's the party line? Is the Bureau at least embarrassed?"

"To them he's just a cranky, eccentric old ancestor." She did not mention that Hoover's spawn seemed to her unchanged from their historical image—the same dark-suited bodies and mannequin-like deportment, the men and women, what few women there were, still marching out of the same mold.

Aimee turned onto Massachusetts Avenue. Kate gazed at the varied architecture along this street, famed in part as home to many foreign embassies, its buildings ranging from modern to white marble Renaissance, from plain brick to ornate Victorian. How different from the stucco pastels of her own Los Angeles, the red Spanish tile roofs, the extravagant, evergreen foliage, and the graffiti marching across the sun-splashed city, encroaching on its wealthiest areas as inexorably as kudzu in the South.

"How'd the session go today?"

Kate shrugged. "Different location, same subject matter. Got trapped afterward by a sister from Chicago wanting to know if homophobia at LAPD is any less with Daryl Gates gone and Mitch Grobeson winning his discrimination suit.''

"What did you tell her?''

"That Chief Williams has yet to show he's got a backbone, and Mitch Grobeson's at Hollywood Division still trying to part the Red Sea.''

Aimee chuckled. "Chicago any better?''

"Nope.''

Mist began to obscure the windshield; Aimee sluiced it clear with a click on and off of the wipers. "So what did you learn today?''

"More trends, more stats. Lots of numbers.'' Aimee's disquiet over police work was burdensome enough without dropping any hints about the seminar's details of ritual torture and ghoulish dismemberment. Again Kate ran a hand down Aimee's thigh. "What's on for tonight?''

Aimee clicked the wipers on and off again. "If it doesn't fucking rain, dinner at the Indian place down the street, a stroll around Dupont Circle. How does that sound?''

"Great.'' She understood Aimee's fascination with the city—she had once felt that way herself—but she had not been looking forward to another round of Aimee's enthusiastic tourism. The upcoming reunion would draw enough emotion out of her without further invasions into her stock of memories.

Aimee said, "So tomorrow's the big day.''

Her mood instantly deflating, Kate did not answer. She thought churlishly that at least Aimee had not as yet suggested a visit to the Wall.

The subdued sign for the colonial-style *Inn on Liberty*

Square came into view, and Aimee, smiling, pulled into the covered entrance to the parking lot at the rear of the Inn. "*Finally* I get to meet up with some of your past."

"You and me both," Kate said, trying to recover her equanimity.

As she got out of the car, she looked more closely at Aimee's new sweatshirt, discerning the logo, a basketball on a bullet-like trajectory through a basket. The Washington Bullets. Bullets, for God's sake. This charnel house of a city even called one of its sports teams the Bullets.

Aimee used her room key to unlock the double doors that led from the parking lot into a small, plain lobby, and turned the same key in another lock to summon the elevator. Kate unbuttoned her raincoat, glanced at herself in the mirrored wall at the back of the elevator to glumly confirm that sitting all day had terminally wrinkled her jacket and pants. Maybe she could get away with wearing jeans and a jacket to dinner.

The elevator door opened onto the second floor. A tall, lanky male in faded jeans and a jean jacket was striding down the corridor toward them. Kate recognized him and greeted him coolly: "Hello again, Woody."

They had exchanged brief greetings that morning in the hotel lobby. Her previous dislike for him had returned undiminished, and she suspected he felt the same way toward her. "Aimee, this is Woody Hampton, one of the men I served with in—"

"A pleasure, pretty woman," Woody interrupted

Kate, "and I do mean a pleasure." He pumped Aimee's hand.

"Nice to meet you," Aimee said, deftly extracting her hand. "See you at the party." She walked on down the navy blue carpeted hallway.

Following her, Kate smiled, thinking how often she wished she could slip a paper bag over Aimee's head because of the attention she drew. This was not one of those times. Aimee had maneuvered their presence here; therefore she deserved Woody Hampton, and whatever else happened this weekend.

Kate shot the dead bolt into place on their room door, moved on down the hallway and tossed her briefcase and shoulder bag onto the bed, then shrugged out of the raincoat and came back to the closet and hung it up. Aimee reached for her. "Hello, grump," she said, nuzzling her throat.

Kate sighed, her resentment releasing her. "Hello, sweetheart." She took her into her arms, kissed her forehead, inhaling the light musk of her hair.

CRACK!

At the same instant, glass shattering. Their hotel room window. Aimee broke away from her. "What—"

"Down!"

The order was purely reflexive; Kate had already dragged Aimee down to the floor. She covered Aimee with her own body, flinching as three more cracks in rapid succession split the air to more splintering of glass.

Aimee struggled beneath her. "What the *hell*—"

"Hold still," Kate hissed.

After several long beats of silence, Kate heard a door

flung open and a deep male voice in the hallway. Angling her body toward the door, Kate carefully rolled off Aimee.

"Aimee, *crawl*. Into the bathroom." The bathroom was right beside them.

Aimee scrambled into it, leaped to her feet, poked her head out into the room's hallway. "Shit! Somebody shot out the window!"

"Get your head *back*!" Did she have no sense at all? "For God's sake, Aimee!"

Kate was crawling toward the bed, and her shoulder bag, and her gun.

A pounding on the door. "Everybody okay in there?" More pounding.

Aimee sprang out of the bathroom, fumbled with the dead bolt on the door.

"*Aimee!*" Kate screamed. She leaped for her shoulder bag, yanked out her gun, and whirled back to the door in a crouch, the gun in a two-handed grip as Aimee flung the door open.

"Hey!" A tall African-American man stood there, clad in sweatpants, his eyes widening at the sight of the .38 leveled at his eyes. "Good God Almighty." The voice was deep bass. He extended his hands, palms up, his bare chest glistening in the light from the hallway. "Hey."

Kate lowered her gun to his kneecaps, and moved toward the door, still holding the weapon in both hands. "Aimee," she commanded, "call nine-one-one. Tell them we have a shooter in the hotel."

Aimee stood gaping from the fissures in the door to the ones in the window. "The door . . . the shots went right through the door and out the window—"

"*Hurry.*"

Aimee rushed for the phone.

Peering first to her left, Kate edged into the hallway. She knew a stairway was to her right; their room was the last one along this hallway. Several people in various stages of dress and undress had come out of their rooms, none of them from the reunion group, or at least not familiar to Kate. At the sight of her and her gun they ducked back into their rooms and slammed their doors.

She said to the African-American man, "What did you see?"

"Nothing. Nobody."

"Nothing at all?"

"Not a soul. I'm right across the hall, heard the shots, came out of my room, saw the bullet holes in your door—"

She interrupted him with a raised hand and moved down the hallway, inspecting it for bullet damage, scrutinizing the blue and white flocked wallpaper, the dark blue room doors, the ceiling.

She returned to the African-American man. "What's your name?"

His eyes again on her gun, he answered, "John Stafford."

"Mr. Stafford, you're a brave man," Kate said, shoving the gun into the waistband of her pants. A brave man, she judged, but a foolish one.

He said in his deep voice, "This doesn't happen where I come from."

"Where is that?"

"Oklahoma City."

She extended a hand. "Kate Delafield. I'm a police officer. Los Angeles."

He looked relieved. And perplexed. Shaking her hand, he peered down into her face. "What's going on? Somebody after you here in Washington?" He managed a faint grin. "I'm on a movie set?"

"Not that I know of," she answered with a wry smile, and then turned to briefly inspect the damage to her own door. Hearing sirens—at least four or five, she judged—she moved down the hallway to the lighted EXIT sign and the stairway door. Its handle was a bar type, and at the point farthest from the doorjamb she carefully pushed down on the bar. Gun in hand once again, she braced the door open with a knee. The staircase looked empty. She let the door swing shut, again stuffed the gun into her waistband.

"Ran down there, didn't he," John Stafford offered.

Kate nodded. "Probably. Or into one of the rooms along this floor."

"Not likely. Not enough time, unless he's in the room right next to you."

Melanie Shaw was in that room. She and Aimee had spent the day together. Either Melanie was not there now or had not come out despite all the commotion. Kate was looking reflectively at the room when Aimee called, "Cops just pulled up in front." She came out of the hotel room. "I forgot to tell them you're police. They won't be happy to see that gun."

Shit, Kate thought. "It'll be okay," she said. She could hear the gurgle-clank of the elevator. "The two of you get back in your rooms."

Kate turned toward the elevator and kept her hands extended before her, hoping these D.C. Metro cops weren't trigger-happy.

The elevator doors opened and out stepped a man and a woman in dark blue uniforms with light blue shirts. Both police officers were African-American, both were resting a hand on the handles of their unsnapped weapons. They immediately backed against the wall, drawing their guns as Kate called in a loud, clear voice: "Police officer! LAPD, Wilshire Division Homicide."

Weapon in hand but pointed slightly downward, the woman moved slowly and carefully, ahead of the man. Kate held her hands stationary as the officers reached her. Then she said, "If you'll give me just a moment, I'll get my identification from the hotel room."

The female officer reached to Kate and deftly removed the gun from Kate's belt. "You just do that," she said.

2

THE woman officer took Kate's ID and inspected it, her narrow-eyed glance shifting from the photo on the ID back to Kate.

The stairway door was pushed open; two police officers, guns drawn, peered into the hallway. "Under control here," the woman officer told them.

"We're checking every floor, Jill," one of the officers said, and withdrew back into the stairway.

The woman returned Kate's gun along with her ID, holstered her own gun.

Kate stowed the gun back in her waistband. She liked this young woman's crisp appearance and her flair, and most of all, her judgment.

"What's the story here?" said the male officer, stuffing his gun back into his holster.

"We—Aimee and I—were out all day," Kate said. "We were back less than a minute, I heard the first shot, heard the window glass go. Three more shots, all of them into the room. Maybe ten seconds later the guy across the hall pounds on the door. I come out into the hallway. See just him and some apparent onlookers. He claims he saw no one in the hallway when he came out."

"Hear any shots from anywhere else in the hotel?"

"No."

"From the street?"

"No."

The woman officer said brusquely, "I'm Jill Manners, Kate. My partner's Rudy Doyle."

She moved off down the hallway before Kate could respond. At the door of Kate's room she beckoned for Kate and Rudy Doyle to join her. "Notice anything different about these bullet holes?" she asked.

"Big," Rudy said. "Big caliber ammo."

"They're high," Kate said.

Jill raised a hand until it was flush with the bullet holes—well over her head. "Yeah. High."

"So the guy shot up," Rudy said, hooking his thumbs over his gun belt.

"Look, Rudy—it's a hollow door. There's a lot of damage, but you can still see bullet entry and exit are level. Somebody held a gun high over their head. No way those shots could hit you unless you were seven feet tall."

Jill walked on into the room and down the hallway— Kate and Rudy following—and headed directly over to the window. Aimee, who was sitting on the bed leaning back on her elbows, looked on with interest. "Aimee Grant," Kate said in introduction.

"We'll speak to you in just a few minutes, Ms. Grant," Jill said courteously.

Aimee said, with a faint grin at Kate, "I guess I know the drill."

Not much of it, Kate thought dourly, remembering Aimee's rash behavior after the shots were fired.

Jill studied the large hole, the network of cracks radiating from it. Rudy Doyle, Kate noted, was watching Aimee with his hands on his bulky hips. With a nod to Aimee, Jill led the group back out of the room.

John Stafford had come out into the hallway. Kate said, "This gentleman is John Stafford."

Jill Manners said, "If you'd be kind enough to just step back into your room, Mr. Stafford, we'll speak to you in a few minutes."

Stafford backed slowly into his room, inspecting Jill Manners from head to foot with an approving smile until his door closed.

Kate and the two officers moved down the hallway, away from the two hotel rooms and out of earshot of either Stafford or Aimee. Jill Manners pulled a spiral notebook and pen out of her back pocket. "Please call us Jill and Rudy," Jill said amid her rapid note taking.

Rudy nodded his assent. Kate relaxed slightly, appreciating this limited acceptance of her as a colleague.

"Any ideas, Kate?" Rudy asked, scratching a mustache that had been shaved to pencil-thinness.

Kate shrugged. Random violence, she supposed, the kind that could touch anybody anywhere in this country. But it wasn't her place to suggest that to these D.C. cops.

"Somebody mad at you?" Rudy suggested. "Somebody you put away?"

"Why take a plane to Washington and shoot through a hotel room door?" Then she answered her own question: maybe somebody wanted to play with her first. It would be easier here, away from her own territory and with the added element of surprise . . . No, she chastised herself, that was crazy, her imagination was running away with her.

Jill asked, pen poised over her notebook, "What are you doing in D.C.?"

"An FBI seminar on criminal profiling." Some of those criminal profiles no doubt accounting for her overactive imagination. She added, "Along with a reunion of some vets I served with."

"At the Gulf?"

"Thank you," Kate said, smiling. "Vietnam."

"Really. My father was there. Who with?"

"Second Battalion, First Marines."

"My dad was Army," Jill Manners said. "Chu Lai."

"Da Nang," said Kate. "What year?"

"Sixty-eight."

Kate nodded. "Me too, and part of sixty-nine. The worst time."

"Yeah. He got a leg blown off."

"I came in just after Tet. Your father helped make it safer. Where—"

Rudy interrupted impatiently, "Any of these ex-Marines still playing with guns?"

Rude Rudy, Kate thought. "I haven't seen any of them for more than two decades," she said. And she wouldn't have this time either, if it hadn't been for Aimee.

Rudy said to Kate, "Then this is some kind of a joke, right? A Marine buddy's idea of a welcome salute?"

"Some joke," Kate said in a short tone. She did not like Rudy Doyle, and she liked even less what he had just said. "No one I knew over there would do anything

like this." Not precisely true. Back then, they would
have. Surely they wouldn't now. . . .

"You're telling me this hotel is crawling with ex-
Marines, some of 'em for sure have to be packing firepower—"

"Maybe it's some crystal freak," Jill said. "Out en-
tertaining himself."

Kate nodded. "Kids today—the world's their shooting gallery." She wanted to believe Jill's theory. Or
even Rudy's, for that matter. To ease the prickling sen-
sation between her shoulder blades.

"Doesn't figure," Rudy said. "A druggie'd shoot up
the whole hallway, not just this door. Looks to me like
somebody was waiting for you to come back here. I
figure somebody's giving you a hello. Or some other
kind of message."

He strode toward the EXIT sign over the hallway
stairs, Jill and Kate following, and shoved open the
door before Kate could get her mouth open to utter
more than a strangled sound.

"Rudy, you dipshit," Jill said.

"Oh, right," he said, hitting himself in the forehead.
"We're gonna track who did this with fingerprints.
And then we're gonna find a way to prove it, with no
witnesses." He scrubbed his hand contemptuously
along the bar handle of the door. "Maybe LAPD's got
time to fart down a chimney . . ."

Kate looked at him in silence. The nonchalant body
language, the shoes in need of polish, the clip-on tie
hanging from one side of the shirt collar, the uniform
pants lengthened by the gut hanging over his gun belt.
His partner, on the other hand—the points of her

light blue shirt were starched crispness, her uniform neat on her full-figured and well-conditioned-looking body. Rudy said to Kate, "What about your hallway neighbor, this Stafford?"

"A do-gooder," she responded. "He doesn't figure to have anything to do with this."

"We'll still talk to him. And your . . . girlfriend."

"Of course," Kate said, her dislike for him solidifying.

"Of course as a professional courtesy," Jill said, "we'll—"

"I'll leave it to you and your partner," Kate said. She would do her own checking into this without any help or interference from either of them.

Jill said, "We're searching the building, we'll look outside for discharged bullets, dispatch units around the neighborhood, but not much probability there." She pulled a card out of a pocket in her notebook. "We'll be in touch when we know something. But call me. Anytime." Kate heard apology in her tone. "Anything I can do while you're in town, be glad to hear from you."

"I appreciate it," Kate said. "Let me get you one of my own cards. And put this gun back out of sight. I always break my gun down as soon as I get home, I just didn't have time before the shooting started here."

"I hear it's a real pain to travel with one," Rudy observed.

Kate nodded. "The FAA needed a letter from my captain stating my duty assignment, the gun had to be unloaded and packed in a gun travel box and locked in a hard-sided suitcase, the airport police checked it through and marked it with orange and black tape."

"Right," Jill said, "so any terrorist on board can go right to it."

Kate joined in their chuckles. "They don't allow guns into New York City, period. Too bad I wasn't going there." No, she would take that back. She was glad she had brought her gun to Washington, D.C.

Hands on his hips, Rudy asked, "How long you been in Homicide?"

"Twelve years."

He greeted this information with slightly elevated eyebrows, then asked, "You in the Division with the O. J. case?"

She smothered a groan. She was sick sick sick of the questions about the O. J. Simpson case. "That particular circus is playing under West L.A. Division's big top." And in Parker Center. Poor Vannatter and Lange . . . she wouldn't be in their shoes if someone offered her a win in the lottery.

"You know any of those cops we see on TV? That Fuhrman turd, is he—"

"He's retired, I knew him only to say hello to," she said, hoping to short-circuit any assumption that she had inside gossip on the case. God, the obsession with this case, particularly among all the police officers she knew.

"So what's the story? Is O. J. guilty?"

"DNA evidence against him is stacked to the ceiling." She shrugged. "Which doesn't mean he'll be convicted."

"Yeah, right. Even videotape wasn't good enough

for Rodney King. You get caught up in that riot business?''

"Everybody did," she said with feeling. "Every police officer in the entire city was on standby alert.''

She had been called in at dusk as media reports filled the airways and a pall of smoke spread over the city. In full uniform plus riot gear, she had driven a black-and-white along with three other officers, shotguns across their laps to protect themselves as well as the city, assigned to patrol the eastern perimeter of Wilshire Division. The entire night and following day had been a nightmare of fires on the horizon and listening to the spreading devastation reported over the police radio.

She had come home to find Aimee hollow-eyed from worry and lack of sleep . . . "A terrible, ugly time, a huge bla—'' She shifted gears as she realized that she had forgotten, in the focus of memory, that these two were African-American police officers. "A very bad business that hurt all of us. We haven't recovered yet, I don't know when or if we can.''

"Some nutball of a town you live in," Rudy said amiably.

Kate said without a trace of irony, "Absolutely no comparison with your paragon of a city.''

Jill laughed, and Kate felt grateful for it. The woman looked to be only in her twenties—too young to have such tense wariness in the posture of her body, such tiredness in her eyes, such cynicism in the curve of her mouth.

Jill said to her partner, "Let's go talk to Mr. Stafford.''

*   *   *

"No," Aimee said. She stood with her hands on her hips as Kate finished packing their clothes.

"We could have been killed." Kate snapped the clasps on the suitcase in emphasis. "You've seen a lot of the city by now—"

"A fraction!"

"The seminar's over, let's get on a plane and get out of here. I promise we'll come back—in April, at cherry blossom time."

"I've seen two inches of the city, you've seen hardly anything, it took a congressional act to get you here this time, we won't be back and you know it—"

Kate turned on her. "I can't begin to understand what's in your head. We were *shot* at." She shook an arm toward the door. "Why aren't you *upset*?"

"Kate, look. We weren't hurt. Whoever did this isn't going to be back—"

"How do you know that?"

"Somebody did this as a joke. One of your Marine buddies maybe had too much to drink. That's what the cops think—and you should too," Aimee insisted. "I'm buying it."

"Buy it if you want to. I don't."

"Kate, honey," Aimee pleaded, "what else makes any sense?"

"It could be somebody I helped convict."

"How would anybody know you're here?"

"We could have been followed."

"You mean somebody followed us all the way to Washington, D.C.? That's ridiculous. Why not just hunt you down and kill you in L.A.?"

Aimee thrust her shoulders back, a posture Kate knew all too well. "This isn't the reason you want to go back," Aimee accused her. "You don't want any part of this reunion. Seeing all these people from your past scares the shit out of you."

"Stow it," Kate snapped. "I'm here, aren't I?"

Aimee said scathingly, "This is probably your newest scheme for getting out of it. Maybe you got that Woody creep to—"

"Aimee." Kate pronounced the name in an arctic tone. "Don't trivialize what happened here." She gestured at the bullet-scarred door. "You were between me and the door. You could have been killed. If those bullets were any lower—"

"They weren't. All right, Kate. Go home. I'll stay for the reunion and explain to all the tough-ass Marines and nurses who served with you how some goofball that can't shoot straight scared the big bad cop all the way back to L.A."

Kate sighed. She did dread this reunion. But how to convince Aimee that her instinct to leave had nothing to do with that, and everything to do with her five-alarm warning signals about this shooting . . .

"All right," she said, and picked up the phone and dialed the front desk. "This is Kate Delafield in room two-twenty-two . . . Yes. We'll take your offer of another room . . . Four-sixteen? Thank you."

3

WITH Aimee in the shower of their new room—a top floor suite courtesy of the management—Kate slid her ID case into her pants pocket and let herself quietly out the door.

Entering the stairwell at the end of the hallway, she walked slowly down a narrow metal staircase, its stairs cushioned with sturdy dark brown plastic treads, checking the door at each level. A fire escape landing was visible outside the window at each floor, the diamond-patterned metal shiny with rain. She could smell stale cigarette smoke; someone had been in here, and not all that long ago.

At the bottom of the staircase she entered the lobby, deserted except for the desk clerk, a young blond man wearing a black bow tie on a starched white shirt, not the clerk on duty when she and Aimee had checked in. She nodded to him, then, holding the door ajar, took a moment to survey the layout of the lobby.

The L-shaped reception desk, to her left and along the same wall, faced the front door. Beside the front door, its plate glass panes lacy with rain, stood a bellman's podium and two luggage carts. To the right of the reception desk was the hallway to the elevators, and along that hallway were separate doorways, one to the Inn's restaurant, the door all glass with *The Patriot* inscribed in red, white, and blue letters, the other door solid cherry wood with a drum and bugle embossed in it, under a white-board sign that read *The Concord Room.* This was the Inn's private dining room where the reunion would be held tomorrow.

The Inn, she thought, was really quite pretty. When she and Aimee had first arrived, they had both liked the lobby's charm—the blue and white floral wallpaper, the simple white tiles of the floor, the tasseled royal blue carpet under a paler blue sofa with its two matching armchairs, the cherry wood cocktail table, the tall white pedestal holding a slender, graceful vase filled with stylized artificial flowers.

The clerk had abandoned his sorting of computer sheets and was watching her. She walked over to the reception desk, pulled out her ID case, displayed her badge and ID card.

He looked them over. "Officer Delafield, ah, ah—"

"Kate is fine."

"I hope our most deluxe accommodations are some consolation for you and your friend. I assure you nothing like this has ever happened at the Inn."

"We're comfortable in the new room, we appreciate it."

He asked in a tone of hope, "This shooting upstairs has something to do with you being with the police?"

"I don't know," she said, "but anything's possible. What's your name?"

"David Olson."

"Mr. Olson, this staircase, is it the only one on this side of the building?"

"Right." His long, bony fingers smoothing and aligning the sheets of computer paper, he glanced down as if working on them would be far more preferable to talking to her. His cool expression and distant manner, Kate judged, had little to do with her as a police officer questioning him; he simply lacked the affability one would expect of someone employed to interact with the public in a good, small hotel.

She asked, "How many other staircases are there?"

"One more, leading into the parking lot."

His dark blue eyes were intelligent and he spoke with precision, but Kate tested him. "So, theoretically, someone could take the staircase leading to the lobby, but exit on another floor."

"No, that's not right," he primly corrected her. "Once you're in the staircase, you can't get back out till you get down to the lobby. The doors lock behind you."

This had been her own observation as well. She did not point out that anyone could brace or tape a door open to insure a return from the staircase. "Isn't that dangerous? Couldn't someone be trapped?"

"Inconvenienced, is all. The Inn has only three floors of rooms for guests." He pushed a string of pale hair out of his eyes. "You get stuck in the stairway, you come down into the lobby, take the elevator back to your room. If there's a fire, the windows on each staircase landing are breakable and lead to a fire escape."

She nodded. "What about the other stairway, the one to the parking lot?"

"Same thing. You take that stairway, you exit in the small lobby off the parking lot. If you don't have a key to get back in, you need to go around to the front door."

"But someone could get in through that parking lot door," Kate argued. "Come in when someone was going out, then wait till someone else got out of the elevator."

"Well, theoretically . . ." The desk clerk hesitated, once more gazing down at his papers.

Kate again reached into her pocket, this time dropping Jill Manners' card on the polished cherry wood of the counter. "Please call this Metro Police officer if you have any concerns about talking to me."

He nodded. "I guess it's okay, all of you are the police. We have surveillance on that parking lot lobby. We had a few problems where guests got . . . hassled."

Strong-arm robberies, Kate deduced. The shooting on the second floor was probably not as much of an isolated incident as David Olson claimed. Plus, the Inn staff had been curiously blasé about the fact that four bullets had been pumped through a door on the second floor; to her knowledge no one had come up there except for a bellman who cast a frowning glance at the scarred door and then proceeded to move their luggage to the fourth floor. Other than the initial alarm of the guests on the second floor, there had been no sense of dismay at all in the Inn. These days, it seemed, sirens were part of the white noise of a city; everyone was used to cops and criminal activity, and to buildings turned into fortifications.

The clerk pointed to a screen recessed well back under the counter. "Anyone entering from the parking lot breaks an electronic beam that triggers the video camera and sounds a two-second buzzer up here. We always look to see who it is."

"Efficient," Kate commented. "At about five-thirty this afternoon, who was here in the lobby?"

Olson looked down at his computer sheets, his somber face softening with a faint smile of satisfaction. "Lots of check-ins. Always have them on Fridays." He shook his head. "The police coming in—the check-ins seemed more titillated than concerned."

"Television," Kate said. "Makes everything seem not quite real. What did you tell people?"

He cleared his throat. "That one of the guests had reported a minor disturbance."

Kate smiled, then gestured to the staircase she had come down to reach the lobby. "Before the police arrived—anybody enter through that door?"

"I didn't see anybody, but I was busy."

"Do you usually check when that door opens?"

"I do. I hear the door open, I check." He added apologetically, "Somebody could have come through, I can't say I wouldn't have missed somebody leaving the Inn. There seems to be no other explanation for how somebody fired those shots and got out of here."

"What about the door to the parking lot?"

"Nobody opened that door around that time."

"You seem very sure."

"The buzzer goes, I look at the monitor. Always. It only takes a second. Look, ah, Kate, my father's a co-owner of the Inn, I pay a lot of attention to what goes on around here, more than most people would."

"I see." That explained why Olson's demeanor did not seem well-matched to his job. But if nepotism had landed him in a position for which he was not ideal, he was obviously trying to make up for it with diligence. "I take it the police officers questioned you pretty closely about this."

"The two black cops? The woman, yes."

"Thank you, Mr. Olson."

"Call me David." He leaned across the counter. "Listen, you and your friend should feel okay here. No need to go back to L.A. and tell—it was a fluky thing, believe me."

"Right," said Kate.

"Have you been out detecting," Aimee said, not a question. Clad in sweatpants and a white pullover, she sat cross-legged on the sofa brushing tangles from her wet hair. She had obviously just finished a very long shower; the suite's living room was permeated with the flowery smells of soap and perfume. "A call came in for you. Torrie Holden. Sounded rushed—I told her you'd call her right back." Taking the Inn's message pad from the coffee table, she got up and handed it to Kate. "What a rotten night. Pouring cats and dogs and little fishes out there."

"It is. Want to have dinner in the Inn restaurant?"

"I don't know," Aimee said disconsolately. "Maybe it'll clear up."

Kate glanced at her watch, calculating the three-hour time difference, then at the number on the pad, which had to be Torrie's home phone number. Torrie must be working on a case and had stopped off on the way home. Sitting at the table near the rain-streaked window, Kate picked up the phone.

"Torrie? It's Kate."

"Hey, Kate. Thanks for calling back. Sorry to bother you on your trip."

"No problem." Torrie's at-home voice vibrated with the same intensity as it did at work. Kate could picture her lean face, the concentration in the dark eyes, the thick, neatly cut and shaped dark hair. A small woman, Torrie always wore a matching jacket and skirt of the plainest cut on the job; Kate wondered what she looked like when she relaxed—assuming she ever eased up on her driven manner—and whether she wore something as casual as jeans.

Torrie asked, "What did the seminar cover?"

Aimee had gone into the bathroom and was drying her hair, and Kate lowered her voice under the buzz of the dryer. "Wednesday and Thursday were at the Behavioral Sciences Unit, Quantico. Today, FBI Headquarters. Sex-mutilation homicide scenarios, replications of organized and disorganized deaths, profiles of crime scenes of the ritual killer, emerging patterns in forensic pathology—"

Torrie's soft whistle interrupted her. "A fun time was had by all."

"Picture *Silence of the Lambs*," Kate said. And some people there, Kate thought, looked as if they could be relatives of Hannibal Lecter in their relishing of all the details of bloodlust and savagery. From her standpoint, psychological profiling was something any experienced investigator automatically did at a crime scene, and the three days of seminar had offered little more than cu-

mulative horror. Sharing even part of the gruesome-
ness of the past three days with a partner, however
junior that partner might be, felt like the lancing of a
boil.

Inhaling the perfumy aromas wafting to her from
the bathroom on air currents from Aimee's dryer, she
glanced over at her securely locked briefcase, remembering her impulse to dump the seminar materials in
the restroom when she was talking to the detective
from Chicago. Not a good idea, inside the FBI Building, and she had thought better of it. She pulled the
top page off the message pad, picked up the Inn-
furnished ballpoint pen. "What's up?"

"You know Centennial Clinic, over on Pico?"

"I know it, never been in it. A hospital-clinic, pretty
small, right?"

"Yeah, it's pediatrics. A child died there, a boy. Eight
years old."

"Oh, Torrie," Kate said softly. Torrie herself was the
single parent of a twelve-year-old girl. "That's a hard
one," Kate commiserated. In her career, most investi-
gations of children's deaths had fallen by the luck of
the draw to other detectives—including this time, apparently. Had she been back there, she undoubtedly
would have been partnered with Torrie, a new D-1 assigned to Wilshire, on this case. Her own investiga-
tions, mostly crib deaths, had been bad enough . . .
SIDS cases left scars on everyone, including the necessarily involved police officers. "A child—it's the kind
of case everybody dreads. I really feel for you, Torrie.
Why were we called in?"

Torrie's sigh transmitted clearly over the line. "A

nurse claims she saw something. Saw a discrepancy in the treatment . . ."

"To the boy." Kate began sketching a hypodermic needle on the message pad.

"To the boy. Close to a vegetable, but not close enough, Kate. Semi-coma, constant pain, constant sedation. Birth defects, some awful progressive nerve degeneration since he was born, on pain meds like you wouldn't believe, morphine drips, a medical history as long as *War and Peace*, his chart looks like some company's annual report."

"God," Kate said. "The poor kid, the poor parents." The anguish in some people's lives continued to amaze her, and to move her.

Torrie's voice was fervent. "The parents—we should all have such a mother and father. Took care of this kid from the moment he was born, visited every day, never been any hope for him, they think their doctor's a saint."

"But the nurse saw something."

"Claims the doctor hurried things along. Like that could be anything but a blessing."

Kate began to shade in the handle of the hypodermic needle, then stopped and inspected her doodle. A psychic connection with this case? She shook her head. "What's the doctor saying?"

"She suggests natural causes. From long-term drug maintenance."

"Mmmh," Kate said. A woman doctor.

"The nurse—God love her honest but dumb young soul—says she understood the prognosis on this kid was that he could live a long time just like he was. And some medical person there did something."

That compassionate medical people sometimes aided in a patient's demise was nothing new, and long before these days of Dr. Jack Kevorkian, but usually such deaths proved difficult to prosecute. "The nurse— does she belong to some sort of fundamentalist fringe group?"

"Not at all," Torrie retorted, and Kate knew that Torrie was reacting defensively because of her own closely held Baptist faith.

As Torrie launched into a description of a young woman fresh out of nurses training, Kate remembered the afternoon she and Torrie had arrested Eddie Marino for the drug-related murder of his cousin, Tony, and Mrs. Marino hysterically reciting the rosary as she clung to a drug-wasted son she would most likely never see again except through the glass of a prison visiting room. Later that day in the parking lot at Wilshire Division, in the emotional aftermath of the arrest, they had compared notes about their own religious upbringing with the openness of two colleagues rubbed raw from the day's events.

Torrie concluded her description of the nurse. Kate asked, "Who are you partnered with?" She braced herself, hoping against hope.

"Leviticus."

Kate closed her eyes. Jack Levering. The transfer from Pacific Division whose specialty was righteous indignation. The worst possible partner on a case like this. "You're doing your job, Torrie?"

"Yeah, I don't know exactly why I'm calling you, except I've been up since two this morning on it, and misery loves company. I guess I thought . . . Shit, I don't know. This Doctor Jimenez isn't one of the bad guys."

"Torrie, just continue to do your job." She should be there, not here, she thought angrily. She should be partnered with Torrie on this emotionally wrenching case. "You need to stay professional."

Torrie sighed. "Autopsy's Monday, and you should hear Tommy's mother about her child having to be cut open on top of everything else he's endured in his young life, and Leviticus telling them they should be grateful to get an answer why their child is dead. . . ."

Kate groaned. If she were with Torrie now, between the two of them they would figure out how best to handle this, and the heartbroken people involved. Anybody could do better than Leviticus.

"We're checking it all out, the kid's medication history, his chart, the drug inventory. Then we'll question the nurse again, and everybody else. People at the clinic may be trying to cover for the doctor—another felony, of course. Kate, it just looks worse and worse."

"Give it your best, Torrie. It's all you can do. I'll call you tomorrow."

Aimee had come back into the room, had heard the last of the conversation.

"What did she think about the shooting here?"

"I didn't tell her," Kate said sheepishly.

"You didn't tell her?" Aimee stared at her. "You're so upset about this you want to leave town? Yet you don't bother to tell your partner about shots fired into your hotel room?''

Kate shrugged.

"You're crazy," Aimee pronounced.

No, Kate thought, just embarrassed.

4

AIMEE kissed Kate on the forehead, then rolled over to her usual sleeping position on her right side, snugly fitting her back and hips into Kate.

Kate lay on her side with an arm around Aimee, a hand filled with the pliant firmness of Aimee's breasts, breathing in essences from Aimee's hair, her face cream, her toothpaste. Aimee's body language conveyed that everything was as usual, but the same note of discordancy continued between them that had constrained their lovemaking for the last week.

They had gone to bed early, after a room-service dinner, the intensifying rain plus the events of the evening having siphoned away Aimee's enthusiasm to spend the time out in the city. Clearly, Aimee was tired tonight—her breathing pattern of sleep had already begun.

Kate released her gently, and rolled over onto her back. A gust of wind rattled rain against the window, and with it came a renewal of resentment that she was in this miserable place at all.

Rain. She hadn't had to think about rain in years. Surely not in Southern California where, except for an occasional aberration, the year was comprised of eight to nine months of predictable sunshine followed by a few months slightly less predictable. Climate might not be a major factor in some people's decision to pull up roots and relocate, but for her it had been decisive in taking leave of Michigan after her service in the Marine Corps. She should be more conciliatory about rain after twenty-some years in California, but this weekend was reviving a number of unwelcome verities.

About memory, mainly. Memory was lawless and illogical. Arbitrary. Capable of bending back on itself like a ribbon. She had learned the nature of memory from Anne's death, eleven years past, and that any event, any piece of her life with Anne, could return with the freshness of yesterday to ambush her, cut her off at the knees.

Rain. She could still remember the wet, steamy island in the South Pacific in that movie she had seen with her father, starring a sultry, vamping Rita Hayworth as a prostitute and Jose Ferrer as a stiff-spined missionary who won her to salvation and then ended up corrupting her again to his sexual desires. Even then Kate's sympathies went with the missionary. The relentless thrum of tropical rain teeming endlessly from palm trees and bamboo huts could unhinge anybody, undermine anyone's moral rectitude.

She'd landed in rain at Tan Son Nhut Airbase. And blackness. The plane's lights extinguishing somewhere over the South China Sea, her apprehension sharpening into fear as the plane fell in a darkness like death onto an invisible landscape. The craft bouncing and shuddering to a halt, then the hatch door opening, and the next sound drumming thunder, silver fists of rain pounding the silver skin of the plane, dull thuds and firefly flashes of distant bomb explosions like accompanying timpani. If there had been any question that she was entering a war zone in a place far outside any previous realm of her experience, the first minutes in Vietnam had answered it. Walking off that plane blind, into heat and teeming rain, onto concussed muddy earth . . .

She rolled from her back onto her side, away from Aimee. Best not to think about any of this, best not to want to know or remember anything about Vietnam. Aimee's intimations of deep psychological meaning to the contrary, Kate's unwillingness to be here at this reunion was no more deep-seated than her unwillingness to dwell on the past. She detested being here, she detested being *forced* to remember. That was all of it— despite what Aimee thought.

The worst mistake she had ever made was to be careless with her past. To have Aimee discover the Vietnam history that lay beyond the cards that arrived each Christmas, the history she'd packed away, the letters and photographs various of her Vietnam companions had sent over the years. The letter from Melanie about this twenty-fifth anniversary of the year they had all served together—that's all Aimee had needed to get on the phone with Melanie and maneuver, no, *trick* Kate into coming here.

It was all academic now. Tomorrow she would see them all again. Rachel. Bernie. Doc. Gabriel. Dacey. Martin. They had been so very young, barely out of their teens when they were all together. She would be an object of curiosity, which she detested, but at least she would not have to explain about Aimee and deal with their immediate reactions. This time they knew the truth of her that they had not known back then. She had directed Aimee to reveal the nature of their relationship to Melanie in vain hope that a homophobic reaction would provide justification for not taking part in the reunion.

What would she find when she saw them again? What changes had come into all their lives?

And Rachel. Rachel . . .

How on earth would she react to Rachel—and Rachel to her?

5

As Aimee preceded Kate out of the elevator, she looked back at Kate in exasperation. Stone-faced, Kate was walking stiffly toward the Concord Room as if toward her own execution. The desk clerk glanced up at them from behind the reception desk, his expression disapproving, perhaps, Aimee surmised, because "I Want to Hold Your Hand" was blaring from the Concord Room, certifying the Inn's blunder in hosting a reunion of Marines.

This was Kate's fault. The woman was absolutely maddening; she would not talk about her feelings except in the vaguest generalities—who could ever guess she would be this distraught? Who could gauge her true level of emotion about anything?

An hour earlier, Kate had quickly approved what Aimee would wear to the reunion—a turquoise silk shirt and white wool pants, tiny pearl earrings—but Kate's indecisiveness over her own clothes had been extraordinary. This woman, dithering over the contents of her garment bag, was the same one who each morning of her professional life pulled an ensemble together in less than thirty seconds. A mild suggestion that the problem would be easily solved had Kate packed her

uniform earned Aimee a look of such withering re-
proof that she had said nothing more.

Now, at the doorway to the reunion, Aimee stepped
aside for Kate. Kate halted and frowned down at her
clothes, a navy blue crew neck sweater with matching
pants and boots. Giving a hitch to the blue-and-white-
striped shirt collar inside the neck of the sweater, she
squared her shoulders, then looked at Aimee.

Torn by Kate's misery, her awkwardness and apprehension, Aimee mustered a confident smile, and
pushed ahead, preceding Kate into the room. A hint
of contrition or remorse at this moment would accomplish nothing, would only add to Kate's agitation.

The room was so hazy with cigarette smoke, so pun-
gent with overtones of floral perfume, that it challenged Aimee's benchmark—the asphyxiating hour
she had spent in a crowded smoker car on a commuter
train with her parents when she was ten. Approxi-
mately twenty-five guests, two thirds of them men, were
clad mostly in military garb; a few women wore cocktail
dresses. Drinks in hand, they stood in animated clus-
ters of five or six, their energized conversational buzz
signifying people excited to be together.

Along the far wall a white banner with cutouts
painted to represent charred bullet holes read: DA
NANG, GATEWAY TO HEAVEN. Three circular tables, each
separately covered with a red, white, or blue tablecloth,
had been set for dinner; a rectangular table decorated
with red, white, and blue bunting held plates of
cheeses and pâtés, crudités and crackers and dips, as
well as a tape deck that blared the Beatles' song. A bar

had been set up; five people had lined up for service from an active attendant.

"As I live and breathe . . . Captain Delafield!"

"Doc Coleman! How you doing, Doc?" Kate had recognized the voice, exclaiming the words as she spun around to an elf of a man coming up on her left. Kate's face froze for only an instant; her surprise at his appearance was evident to Aimee only because she knew Kate's skill at guarding her facial reactions.

Aimee gazed with amusement at this vision of at least three cycles of male culture and fashion. His concave chest sported a small embroidered vest over a gray T-shirt; his pear-shaped hips and midriff were clasped by shiny black pants; his small feet were shod in pointed cowboy boots. Neck-length hair was springy gray-white; wire-rimmed granny glasses scarcely covered his eyeballs. His left ear held three gold stud earrings.

Shifting a glass of red wine to his left hand, which already held a cigarette forked between two fingers, he pumped Kate's hand. "Kate, you look great, just great."

"You look fantastic, Doc," Kate answered, and smiled; Aimee knew she meant the term literally.

Taking a sip of his wine, Doc peered at Kate out of sagacious blue-green eyes. "You always were such a sly one."

"Sly?" Aimee offered. "Kate Delafield was sly?"

"Sorry, Aimee," Kate said, turning to her in swift apology. "I'd like you to meet Doctor Edward Coleman. Doc, this is Aimee Grant."

A courtly nod. "A pleasure. May I present Maria Coleman, my wife."

Shorter than her husband by almost half a foot, Maria Coleman also held a wineglass, gracefully cupping its base in her palm. A pleasant-faced woman with simply coiffed graying hair, she looked comfortable in her plain forest-green dress and in her body which had eased into middle-age spread. Lively, observant dark eyes took in both Kate and Aimee; her smile conferred warmth.

"Guatemalan," Coleman said. "We're learning each other's language." He grinned at Kate. "One word a week."

"Someone who won't talk back," Kate said. "Finally found your perfect mate, Doc."

The chuckle Kate shared with him contained such complicity that the falling away of twenty-five years' separation was nearly palpable. Why had Kate fretted over this reunion? It was going wonderfully well.

"Katie!"

A heavyset woman less than five feet tall and wearing a bright red cocktail dress and gold sandals grabbed Kate, crushed her in a hug, then shook her as if she were a rag doll.

"Bernie," Kate protested, laughing, pushing at her shoulders, "you'll break my ribs."

"Not these ribs," Bernie said, stepping back and thumping Kate's sides with both hands, "not these ribs ever! Look at you, honey, you still don't look a day over twenty-two!"

Bernie, Aimee thought, didn't look a day younger than sixty despite her dyed jet-black hair. And she had to be in her forties, not much older than Kate. The rouge, sloppy eyeliner, messy eye shadow, and bright lipstick were bad enough, but the heavy powder was merciless bas-relief for the network of lines in her ruddy face.

A little man in a dark suit and tie bobbed in her wake, his egg-shaped bald head glistening under the lights. Bernie flung an arm around his shoulders, almost dislodging the drinks he carried in each hand. "This," she trumpeted, "is my Ralph. Ralph Murphy."

Kate turned to Aimee, her face holding as big a grin as Aimee had ever seen on her. "Aimee, this is Bernadette O'Rourke. I mean Murphy."

"*Every*body calls me Bernie," Bernie said, grabbing Aimee's hand.

Aimee felt an instant liking for her. Slapdash makeup seemed hardly a fault on a woman who was not the kind to notice or care that her red dress clashed audibly with the maroon carpet, who would not mind that the gold chain belt on her dress had missed one of the cloth rungs. "Really glad to meet you, Bernie," she said. Why hadn't Kate kept more closely in touch with this woman?

"Ain't you the beauty," Bernie said to her so offhandedly that it seemed more a statement of the commonplace than a compliment. She took one of the drinks from Ralph and tossed off its mahogany contents. "Ralphie, didn't I tell you about my Katie? Isn't she the grand gal I said she was?"

"Sure is, dear." Ralph looked from Kate to his wife in head-dipping approval that reminded Aimee of a bobbing doll on a dashboard.

As Kate shook hands with him, she asked Bernie, "Are you still in nursing?"

Bernie handed her empty glass back to Ralph. "Get me another, please, sweetie?" She answered Kate, "Am I *ever* still in nursing, honey." She pulled a pack of Salems from her purse and winked at Kate. "The vets at Charleston, they call me Nurse Ratched."

Another voice:"Did I hear the name Delafield?"

Kate did not conceal the softness in her voice or in her face as she said, "Hello there, Gabe. How you doing, Sarge?"

"Just great, Captain." The tall, handsome, muscled man in green military fatigues and matching cap raised his right hand shoulder-high, and Kate met his hand in a grip so strong and hard and sure that it looked as if the two of them had invented it as their own private greeting.

Aimee was entertained by the tableau of Gabe, Doc and his wife, Bernie, and Kate, all standing in silence for a long awkward moment, glances sliding off one another in the manner of people whose urge to stare was barely curbed by politeness. Knowing she had to make her own way among these resurrected ghosts of Kate's past, Aimee extended a hand to Gabe. "Aimee Grant."

"Gabe Bradford. How you doing?"

Accustomed to holding most men's attention, she lost his immediately. "I hear you're a cop," he said to Kate. "In L.A."

"Right."

He took a deep drag from his cigarette, flicked the ashes into the palm of his hand. "How can you stand the place?"

"Gabe, it never rains in Southern California."

More complicity in the smiles that conveyed how much history had been condensed into so few words.

"What about you?"

"Little of this, little of that." He grinned sheepishly. "Right now I'm doing some business with ITEK, an outfit specializing in bartering—"

Kate and Doc and Gabe all burst out laughing. Doc said, "Still a cumshaw operator, eh Gabe?"

Gabe grinned. "Stays in the blood, you know."

Aimee was about to ask what a cumshaw operator was when Doc said, "Listen, we heard about some shots fired into your room—what on earth was that all about?"

"Beats me," Kate said. She added lightly, "I thought maybe it was all of you telling me how glad you were to see me."

Everyone chuckled except Gabe, who said, "You must be some tough cop—if that'd happened to me, I'd have been out of this town on the next plane."

"I'm not the tough one," Kate said, smiling, gesturing to Aimee.

"Did they catch anyone?"

"They're still investigating. They—"

"Kate." A woman had glided up beside Kate, dark-haired, clad in jeans and a green military shirt, the word *Summer* stenciled across a breast pocket.

Her face freezing, Kate turned, but in an exaggerated slow motion that indicated to Aimee the greatest unwillingness. "Hello, Rachel."

Kate's tone was too flat, her face too closed. Hello Rachel indeed. Aimee's hackles rose.

"How are you, Kate?"

"Fine, doing fine." Kate asked with formality, "Are you still in nursing?"

"Yes. Still."

And if your nurse couldn't be the hallowed Dana Delany from *China Beach*, Aimee thought, Rachel would do quite nicely.

"With a few stops and starts here and there," Rachel said. "It wasn't easy for a long time. You look good, Kate."

"So do you, you look great, Rachel."

Great did not do this Rachel woman justice. If you had to wake up in a hospital bed you'd want those warm, compassionate, wise, reassuring, embracing brown eyes gazing down at you . . . If you were in any bed, you'd want to wake up to this woman and those eyes . . .

Feeling as if she were in free fall off a cliff, Aimee took Kate's arm in automatic, instinctive possession. Every advantage she had ever enjoyed because of the fifteen-year age difference between her and Kate seemed to be suddenly dissolving. The consummate maturity of this woman relegated youth to a distinctly inferior position and made good looks irrelevant.

"Introduce me," Aimee said.

But the woman had already reached to her, clasping Aimee's hand in her soft, warm hand. "I'm Rachel Summer."

Of course your name would be Summer, Aimee thought. "Aimee . . . Grant," she said, clearing her throat to get both words out.

"Bring me up to date, Rachel," Kate said. She was completely ignoring Doc, Bernie, and Gabe, who stood in gawky grinning attendance, sipping from their drinks and sucking smoke from their cigarettes. Not to mention Aimee herself, who didn't have even the comfort of a drink much less a cigarette. No one existed in this room for Kate but this Rachel woman.

Rachel said, "I'm back home in Baltimore. Children both married."

"So I heard," Kate said.

Aimee let out a breath of relief. *Married. Straight. Thank God.*

"Did you hear I'm divorced?" Rachel continued. "It's . . . let me think . . . fourteen years now."

She couldn't bear it. "Kate," she said, "why don't I get us a drink?"

"I'd appreciate it. Thank you."

All formality, she was, Aimee thought furiously, stalking off to the bar.

Fishing a twenty-dollar bill out of her purse, she instructed the barman, "A double scotch over ice, a glass of white wine."

"Scotch with a wine chaser," said a male voice approvingly. "That's what I call a drink." The stranger, blond and handsome, with a neat reddish beard, wearing a blue-checked flannel shirt and jeans and cowboy boots, nodded. "Name's Dacey," he said. "How you doing? A beer," he instructed the barman, "anything you got back there's okay."

She took a sip of wine and managed a smile. "I'm Aimee Grant."

"Hi, gorgeous," said another voice from behind her.

The nitwit she'd met yesterday night in the hallway. Woody Hampton, she remembered. In camouflage duds from his cap to his boots, and for God's sake the eagle, globe, and anchor emblem of the Marine Corps tattooed on both biceps. All he needed was an ammunition belt across his chest and a knife between his teeth instead of the stupid cigarette hanging out of the corner of his mouth. "How are you," she said grudgingly.

Woody took a gulp of his tobacco-colored drink. "What's this about your room getting shot up yesterday?"

"You serious?" Dacey said, picking up his bottle of Miller's before the barman could pour it into a glass. "Didn't hear a thing about it."

"Millions didn't," Aimee said. "Somebody welcomed us to the city with a four-bullet salute." She added with a touch of malice, "It happened right after we saw you, Woody."

"They catch anybody? Why would anybody do that? What was it all about?" The intense blue eyes Dacey fixed on her were narrowed.

"Actually, we have no idea," she said, appreciating his concern and thinking that a saving grace about a beard was that it could effectively frame a man's eyes and his mouth, especially eyes as striking and lips as sensual as Dacey's.

Woody said, "What's this stuff I hear about you and Kate?"

Her hackles once again rising, she said icily, "What is it that you hear?"

"Woody—" Dacey began.

Woody ignored him. "You actually belong with her?"

"Belong?" she repeated.

"Woody, you're a total jerk," Dacey stated.

Woody continued as if he had not heard a word from Dacey. "Yeah. Meaning—"

"Nice to meet you," she said to Dacey, and strode away with her drinks as the tape deck began "A Hard Day's Night." Kate was right, it was the dumbest idea on earth to come here. These people, smoking like factories and soaking up hard liquor like suction cups, were from the dark ages and belonged right back there with the Beatles.

Kate was *still* talking to Rachel. Gabe and Doc spoke quietly together; Bernie and her Ralphie had drifted away—who could blame them? "Thanks," Kate said, and in two gulps tossed down half of the scotch.

Nervous as a cat she was, hopping around Rachel. There was more history to this Vietnam year, Aimee thought, than she probably wanted to know about.

"Kate, is it true what I hear about you and this good-looker?" said Woody from Aimee's elbow.

Aimee looked at Kate. "I can't believe this."

"I don't care what you've heard," Kate told him, and turned her back on him. Aimee was gratified.

Rachel contemplated Kate with raised eyebrows, then slid the drink out of Kate's unprotesting hand, took a sip, and handed it back with a faint smile. Seething, Aimee switched her stare to Rachel. Who did this woman think she was?

"Woody," Rachel said, "I see you haven't changed a single jungle stripe."

"Still my fighting weight, Miss Florence Nightingale, still get into the uniform just like I did before."

"Still our good old Woody," Rachel said.

Woody's obliviousness to Rachel's cool contempt reminded Aimee of boys she had known at Palisades
High School, so persistent and obtuse in their siege of
a desired female that any notion that the female might
actually be indifferent to them was consigned to im-
possibility.

"Hello, everybody," said a new voice.

"Martin," Doc Coleman said, giving the name a mel-
lifluous, enthusiastic extra syllable, his eyes lighted with
distinct pleasure. "It's good to see you, really good, my
man. How are you doing?"

Martin, wearing gray slacks, a white polo shirt, and
black blazer, cashmere by the look of it, shook Doc's
hand. His thick gray mustache, covering his lips,
twitched as he inspected Doc. "A damn sight better
than you." His voice resonated with disapproval. "That
getup left over from Halloween?"

"No, from sixty-eight," Doc quipped, clearly not taking offense.

Martin turned to Kate. "You, my dear, look fine.
Splendid, in fact."

Kate smiled, distantly, Aimee thought. "Aimee,"
Kate said, "this is Dr. Martin Goldberg."

Aimee shook hands with him, thinking that his
smooth face was well-tanned for this late in the year.
His glance lingered on her and then slid away, as if
she were interesting but in insufficient degree to hold
his attention.

"How are you doing these days, Martin?" Kate inquired politely, formally.

"Walter Reed, Cardiology," he said. "And you?"

Not quite what Kate had asked, Aimee thought. Kate said, "I'm doing fine."

Rachel was looking around the room in obvious indifference to this byplay. "Where's Dacey?"

"Haven't seen him," Kate said.

"I did." Aimee searched the room, guilty that Dacey's attempt at friendliness had been aborted by her anger over Woody. "Maybe he stepped out."

"I'm wondering about Allan Gerlock." Kate took a long draught of her scotch. "I heard he was due in this afternoon."

"We said hello just a little after four," said Gabe. "He was just checking in."

"He's one room over from me," Woody said.

"And he looks great," Gabe added.

Melanie appeared in the doorway, stopping to survey the crowded room. Aimee was unsurprised by her skin-tight black pants and a lilac sweater with a neckline plunging well down into her ample cleavage. Aimee caught her eye and beckoned. Finally, someone she could hang with and talk to, even if Melanie did have to meet and greet every person in the room. Anything was better than this compulsion to cling to Kate. Where had Melanie been, anyway? She was the organizer of this stupid shindig.

Melanie made her way through the noisy crowd toward Aimee, exchanging greetings and bear hugs as she did so, then surprised Aimee by taking her by the arm and saying urgently, "Come on over to the bar."

"Where've you been?" Aimee demanded.

"Hey, I'm always late for everything," Melanie said artlessly. "I've been out running around with Jenny

Griffin all day." She pointed out a tall brunette in a blue pantsuit who was talking to Bernie. "What's this I hear about a shooting outside your room?"

She allowed Melanie to lead her toward the bar. In between Melanie's glad-handing, Aimee went briefly over the events of yesterday. "I called and called you but no answer," Aimee told her. "We just got back when it happened."

"I'm glad I was gone, I'd have shit my pants. I dashed out to get some bourbon," Melanie said, and ordered the same drink, straight up, from the bartender.

Took her one hell of a long time to get back, Aimee thought, glancing over toward Kate to see if she was still talking to Rachel.

Her gaze was arrested by the look of unguarded dismay on Kate's face. Now what was *that* all about? Dacey, the good-looking guy with the beard, had just come up to her. What on earth could he have said to bring such anguish to the face of the most armored woman on earth?

Kate excused herself from Dacey and the rest of the group and fled to the bar. Waiting her turn to give her drink order, she greeted three other male reunion members waiting in line, their camouflage fatigues unable to camouflage their paunches. She could scarcely recognize much less remember the three, but she did her best with small talk. The room had grown noisier; a large, voluble group had gathered around the hors d'oeuvres table.

A billowing white-gray halo of cigarette smoke

clouded the lights of the room, drink glasses sat discarded everywhere, including on the floor, the Beatles' "Penny Lane" rocked from the tape deck. Not much different, she thought, from the various officers' and NCO clubs way back when everybody drank hard, smoked hard, partied hard.

Finally able to order her double scotch on the rocks and another white wine for Aimee, she gulped part of her drink to lay some immediate balm over her nerves.

She glanced at her watch. After seven, almost time for dinner. Where on earth was Allan Gerlock, one of the few worthwhile reasons for her being here? Agitation punctured the effect of the scotch. She needed more help here, all the help she could get. She needed a cigarette. Had not felt in years such a craving to pull hot sharp rich smoke down into her throat and lungs. She'd bum one off someone this very second, except the dead Anne seemed eerily corporeal, as if she'd step right through the doorway and reproach her with a look, just like she used to do before Kate gave up smoking for her. She might be over Anne, not even think about her much anymore, yet sometimes Anne's very *nothingness* spiked so deep that it was as if her flaming death on the Hollywood Freeway had just happened. One more instance of that winding ribbon of time bending back on itself.

Seeing Aimee occupied in conversation with Melanie, she focused on her drink, swirling new patterns into snowy ice that looked like foam packing spheres. Unwilling to stare at anyone in this room, she did look up, then away again, compelled by a dizzying push-pull of fascination and dismay.

She settled her gaze on Aimee and Melanie. Some of the impact of these resurrections from her past could be laid at Melanie's feet. Meeting her three days ago had been reassuring—and misleading. Melanie had seemed so . . . unchanged from the opinionated pin-brain she had always been that she had created in Kate a false expectation: everyone would be equally unchanged, wrinkles added here and there, a few pounds, a little gray hair on everyone, the men a little bald, but no other substantive differences.

Supposedly seasoned in realism by twelve years as a homicide detective, she could not believe her naiveté, her idiocy. Look at them, she ordered herself, take this in like you would a crime scene.

Bernie. Bernie looked a thousand years old.

What was she to make of Doc? What in God's name had become of the tower of brash certainty whom she and Rachel had called Ben Casey behind his back?

Gabe looked . . . she did not know what in the world to make of Gabe. How could Gabe Bradford of all people turn up here wearing military fatigues after sending her letters haunted with bitterness about the war?

Martin. Nothing left of the Martin she knew, nothing even close to that gentle man who wore his yarmulke in the operating room. Everything gone, even the intensity in his dark eyes, those young-old eyes of Nam had become . . . she did not know what. Inscrutable. Opaque.

And Woody. The embodiment back then of the young lords of the Corps who placed women on the same shelf as Kleenex or toilet tissue, less valuable than a good hunting dog. Woody Hampton had been everything she had come to despise in the Marine Corps, and every disgusting trait he'd ever had back then had obviously solidified; he was now cast in bronze as a turd.

Rachel. Rachel, for God's sake. Rachel. Of all people she should not stare at. A primary reason she had dreaded coming here was the closely held precious memory of Rachel that she wanted to keep intact. The Rachel that Vietnam had created would of necessity be extinguished by the years. But everything she had worshipped about Rachel, her compassion, intelligence, beauty, seemed deepened, as if age had burnished it all, and had added another layer—but in the formalities of their meeting she could not as yet discern the components of that new layer . . .

The worst moment by far was seeing Dacey. Odd that he would not be in fatigues or his dress blues when he had been the poster boy Marine. That beard. How ridiculous to be so upset over a beard, ridiculous to think it was an ax chop at the conviction she'd held dear for twenty-five years, that Cap was alive. He could still be alive. But . . . one of the possibilities had been that Cap and Dacey . . . But Cap had been so vehement in his abhorrence of hairy male bodies and bearded faces, Cap would never stand for that beard.

Aimee. Observing everything like a vulture hovering over roadkill. Maybe she was being harsh, but she hoped Aimee would now be satisfied. Not for the first time she asked herself why Aimee couldn't just leave matters alone. Like Anne had. Anne had asked questions, lots of questions, but in a framework of accepting Kate's description of Vietnam as a year and twenty days

in limbo, at the rear of the war, in charge of the two
staff NCOs and two clerks assigned to Supply, away
from infantry assaults and air strikes, her only enemies
rain and heat and boring routine. But not Aimee.

Aimee's questions had been intermittent and casual,
as if each question had just occurred to her, yet slanted
in the way you'd expect from someone who made her
living as a paralegal. The whole gays-in-the-military de-
bate had set her off, and into the private areas Kate
did not want exhumed— *What were the gay people like over
there? How did you protect yourself? What would you have
done if the investigators had come after you?*—the kind of
tricky questions you'd find in a cross-examination. And
in the end, treating Kate's flat assertion that Vietnam
was no big deal as a bluff to be called. Plotting with
Melanie, and engineering Kate's presence here just so
she could sniff around for herself in the past that was
Kate's own, the past whose ashes Kate had every right
to preserve undisturbed.

Aimee accepted the glass of wine from Kate with a
smile, not so much for the wine as in relief that she
had finally left Rachel.

Aimee said, "What's up with Dacey?"

"Dacey?" Kate's perplexity looked genuine.

"Dacey," Aimee repeated. "You looked upset by
whatever he said to you."

"He didn't say anything that upset me," Kate said.

Aimee shrugged. *I saw what I saw.* Sometimes Kate
could make her doubt her own sanity.

The Beatles tape was turned off, a sprightly piano
version of "Hotel California" came out of a speaker in

the acoustic tile ceiling; a waiter entered bearing a large tray of salads.

Aimee had checked the place cards on the tables to see where she and Kate were seated. Kate had been positioned between Gabe Bradford and someone named Ken Kowalski, while she herself was at the same table but between Bernie and Doc. At least Kate would not be sitting with Rachel, who was evidently at another table.

Then, as the milling crowd arrived at the tables, Aimee saw Rachel Summer switch a place card, presumably her own, with Ken Kowalski's.

Rachel noticed Aimee noticing her. "You don't mind, do you? It's been a long time since I saw Kate, we have a lot to catch up on, you're not seated by her anyway."

Aimee managed a smile. "You're asking the wrong person."

What else could she say?

6

ACCOMPANIED by Bernie, Kate entered the lobby of the Inn and nodded to David Olson at the desk, who surveyed Bernie from head to foot, then gave both of them an astringent smile. "Sounds like you're all having a good time back there," he said dourly.

"Terrific." Bernie gave him a four-finger wave.

In the elevator, as Bernie chattered about Allan being legendary in Nam as a reluctant riser, some mornings having to be pulled from his bunk and virtually set on his feet, Kate stared at herself in the mirrored back wall as if inspecting a mysterious stranger. She pressed her head against the glass trying to cool the heat in her face, dizzy from the potent cigarette smoke and heavy floral perfumes of the Concord Room. She'd asked to accompany Bernie, saying it would give her a chance for a personal meeting with Allan away from the chaotic presence of the group, seizing on this reason to get away and regroup, to make sure her roiling stomach dealt successfully with her few bites of dinner. She'd had too much scotch, too fast. Rachel Summer, in any amount, was too much. And the reunion itself was altogether too much.

Everyone hauling out pictures of children and

spouses and lovers, that was okay. But learning about people not at the reunion—nurses Paula Davis and Jane Cambridge dead of cancer, dustoff pilot Will Maloney from a heart attack, First Lieutenant Steve Taylor a suicide by gunshot, and Captain Bobby Davidson in a single-fatality auto accident that sounded very like it could be suicide as well. Martin relating what he considered all the "success" stories had added no leavening comfort. Mike in a high position at Microsoft, Phil making a name for himself in Milwaukee politics, Jean running a hospital in Anchorage, Connie a real estate mogul in Dallas—they were no compensation for those other vanished men and women who had managed to safely escape Vietnam only to die young anyway, who would remain forever youthful in her memory, the loss of them a grief that seemed to be settling permanently at the bottom of her rib cage.

Bernie knocked several times on the hotel room door, then thumped it with her fist. "Allan, it's Bernie O'Rourke. Allan, it's Bernie." She put an ear to the door. Kate could hear no sound of a shower going, no sound at all.

"There's a good reason for this," Bernie said. But she and Kate hurried to the elevator and back down to the desk where Kate took over.

"David," she said, "Allan Gerlock in room two-twelve. Do you remember him?"

"Of course. I checked him in."

"Did you see him leave?"

"Haven't seen him at all." Three vertical creases between his eyes deepened, looking like fork tines as he peered from Kate to Bernie and back again. "I've been on the desk since three-thirty."

"Please ring him," Kate said.

While they waited, he said in a hopeful tone, "He could be in someone else's room."

Or in his own, having a heart attack, Kate thought.

"Everyone except him is at the reunion," Bernie told him.

"David," Kate said, "please open his room so we can make sure he's all right."

"Oh, Moses," he sighed, the fork tines reappearing. "Gloria," he called into a small office behind the reception desk. "Gloria, could you take the front a few minutes?"

Gloria grumbled assent and came out, a young, slump-shouldered, dishwater blonde. Olson unlocked a drawer and selected a plastic card key, came out from behind his counter and preceded Kate and Bernie to the elevators.

At room 212 he gave the door a long, heavy-knuckled rap. "Mr. Gerlock, it's the management. Mr. Gerlock . . ."

With a head shake and a long-suffering sigh that Kate knew was a mask for apprehension, he fumbled the card key into the slot and opened the door. The only light in the room emanated from the bathroom. Kate attempted to go past him, but he blocked her. "Mr. Gerlock," he called, "Mr. Gerlock, it's the management . . ."

Stepping into the room, Bernie following him, he moved down the hallway and peered into the bathroom.

"Uuhh . . . Moses . . ."

"Oh, Jesus," Bernie said. "Katie, it's Allan."

Bracing the room door open with her shoulder bag, Kate shouldered past them both and in one glance took in the partially clad, blood-smeared body on the bathroom floor, the pools and stains of blood on the pale gray tiles of the floor, the grayish pallor, the unmistakably fatal gash in the throat, the absence of any visible instrument that might have caused this death.

"David," she said, "put your hands in your pockets. Bernie, don't move."

Bernie froze in her tracks. Olson, his face chalky, his Adam's apple bobbing, stared at her in bewilderment, but obeyed.

Acutely aware of the absence of her gun, Kate inched further into the shadowy room. In the light cast from the bathroom she could see that the sliding closet door was open; a black garment bag hung within. A set of camouflage fatigues lay neatly arranged on the bed, boots on the floor beside it. The room looked tidy, and more importantly, empty of any other person or persons.

"Now leave, both of you." Her knees felt as if someone had struck them from behind. But her police mind had switched into automatic pilot. "Retrace your footsteps, don't touch anything. David, don't take your hands from your pockets." Olson had had to open the door to get in, but recoverable prints might be on the inside doorknob.

"Bernie, take David downstairs." Bernie was a perfect recruit to carry out instructions; her training and experience would have kicked her into automatic pilot just as Kate's had. "Call nine-one-one."

"Got it," Bernie said briskly, taking Olson's arm.

Audibly swallowing, he glanced toward the phone on the desk near the window.

"We can't touch anything in this room, David. Bernie, tell them a man is dead, tell them to send the police, tell them a visiting police officer is protecting the scene. Got that?"

"Got it."

Olson tried to speak, coughed, recovered his voice enough to croak, "What next . . . Moses, what next . . ."

As Bernie guided him carefully out the door, Kate said, "The front door to the hotel—can you close it off?"

Olson nodded and mumbled, "After this we might as well padlock it."

"Lock it while Bernie makes the call," she ordered. "Lock off the elevator and the entrance from the parking lot too, if you can. Don't let anyone in or out till the police come. It's all right, David, everything will be okay."

She followed them to the doorway, watched Bernie walking him down the hallway and into the elevator. Then Kate sucked in her breath, stuffed her hands into her jacket pockets, and moved carefully back into the room, retracing as best she could her original path.

It occurred to her that this was the first time she had ever been alone at what appeared to be a homicide. Always before she had been accompanied by a partner, with police officers preceding them both and securing the environment. For the first time she fully appreciated the emotional support of having others present at a death scene, especially one with so much personal impact.

She closed her eyes for a moment, trying to steady herself, then took in the carnage in the bathroom, forcing herself to study the scene. "What in the hell happened here," she muttered, to hear her own voice.

Allan Gerlock, head and chest outlined by a border of blood, clad only in trousers tan-colored in the areas not blood-saturated, lay on his right side about five feet away from her in a fetal position on the gray tiles, just in front of the sink. His face was turned toward her, his wide thin lips in the same slack, downturned shape as that other huge, red-lipped mouth newly incised into his throat. His gore-coated left hand had fallen away from his throat in testimony to the futility of trying to stanch the gush from that mouth.

He had been shaving; white foam mottled by red droplets had partially dried on his cheeks, and a foam-coated, silver-handled straight razor lay up against the side of the bathtub. Blood spattered the white cabinets, probably from Allan Gerlock's death throes, and, before his heart had ceased pumping it from his body, had collected in irregular, dully gleaming dark pools; a ruby river had flowed through a channel in the tiles to soak into a thick terry cloth bath mat, shading it the color of pale cherries. A pristine white bath towel lay in a damp rumpled heap behind the stained mat. The room held no particular smell; the metallic scent of blood had not yet begun to permeate this small space.

Allan's glazed dark eyes were fixed on his right hand. Its outstretched fingers taut, its index finger coated in blood, the hand was formed into a tent-like claw to protect what lay under it from the encroaching red flood.

Kate stared at the hand. Unless Allan had fallen on a suicide weapon, which appeared unlikely with an innocuous, blood-free razor in full view, this death was a murder. From force of habit, she glanced at her calendar watch: 7:24 p.m., November 19. But she did not have the notebook that was always part of her personal armor at a crime scene. And she lacked the authority, and the means, to begin the process of constructing a shell of protection over the shreds of dignity remaining to this man whose natural span of years had been wrenched away in an act of savagery.

She stood at the door, the imperative rising to impose justice on this crime, outrage filling her as it always did on behalf of any victim. Overriding everything was her anguish that the information this man possessed was irretrievably gone. Through all the years she had resisted meeting him, she had always believed she could find out, if she needed to, the nonofficial details of the day Cap had vanished. Now the opportunity was gone forever.

Her proper course of behavior now was to leave and remain in the hallway to simply guard the scene. This murder was not her case. Absolutely no way was this her case. It would not be her case if it had happened within the confines of Wilshire Division; it would not be assigned to her because of her personal connection to it.

Sucking in her breath, she edged her way into the bathroom, inching with exquisite care along the pools of blood until she could hunker down and stretch out a hand. He was warm to her touch; if his body temperature had dropped, it was by no more than a degree or two. His mature male body appeared to be well-toned; he looked, she thought, to be within five pounds of his ideal weight.

She touched the claw-like hand, braced her thumb and index finger on either side of the palm to lift it. The hand resisted her effort to uncover what lay beneath. Rigor mortis had begun setting in quite early, as it occasionally did in cases of sudden, violent death. I have no business doing this, she thought, then pulled carefully, firmly, on the hand.

Underneath were three letters of the alphabet. Written in the only medium Allan Gerlock had available to him. C, was the first crimson character; A, the second; the third was smeared, perhaps an F. Or a P.

CAP. She stared, confounded.

Cap.

He's saying Cap killed him?

But Cap's . . .

Cap was *alive.* She felt an exhilarated certainty surge through her, as fresh and undiminished as if they were all back again in Da Nang.

The Marine Corps might list Cap as an MIA, missing in action near Khe Sanh up at the Demilitarized Zone, his name on that Wall of over 58,000 names that she had never been able to confront—but she had never conceded that Cap was either missing or dead, and never would, unless and until his bones came back in a box, identified to a certainty and without any guesswork cloaked in scientific claim by the Central Intelligence Lab. She had kept her own suspicions to herself all these years as to why and how he had come up missing. Maybe Dacey was simply no longer part of that equation.

Why would Cap's initials be under Allan's hand? What reason on earth could Cap possibly have had for killing Allan? Unless there was an ocean of history here. History she'd had no part of for twenty-five years.

Sirens, increasing in volume, intruded into her bemusement, and she gently lowered the hand. Olson's call was being answered code three, and by a fleet of vehicles.

Putting her hands back in her pockets, she retraced her path out of the room, then went down the hallway and waited beside the elevator.

Jill Manners soon emerged, followed by Rudy Doyle.

"We have to stop meeting like this," Jill offered, angling a glance past Kate as if she expected to see a corpse in the hallway. Then her gaze focused on Kate's face.

"We're gonna start calling you Dirty Harriet," said Rudy Doyle.

In no mood for their badinage, Kate said flatly, "Room two-twelve."

Rudy strode down the hallway and into Allan Gerlock's room, Kate closely following. "What a mess. Think this guy might be your shooter?" He took a step into the bathroom, without so much as a glance at where he was placing his feet.

"Don't go one inch further. To answer your question, no, I don't."

Rudy's eyes narrowed into dark slits. "You think I

don't know dick?'' His voice was a low snarl.

Yes, she thought. "Automatic," she said. "I'm a homicide cop."

"Not here," he snapped.

But he had backed out of the room to confront her, which was all she wanted.

"Rudy," Jill said, casting an apologetic, placating glance at Kate, "let's get to work. Get this whole floor sealed off.'' She said firmly to Kate, "We'll need you to step outside."

"Of course."

Other officers had arrived and were streaming down the hallway. A tall, portly sergeant conferred with Rudy, looked sharply at Kate, then directed his officers, gesturing to the pathway to the body he presumably wanted set up.

7

FIFTEEN minutes later Sergeant Dix, his broad face expressionless, questioned Kate in her room with cautious deference about her discovery and protection of the death scene, occasionally holding up a hand to slow her so that he could complete his notes of the actions she had selected to reveal.

Then Dix said courteously, "Would you please wait here, Detective, we'll have more questions in a few minutes."

She was not surprised that it was in fact more than an hour before two male detectives made their way to her room, one short and rotund and wearing a sporty tweed jacket and bone-colored pants, his tan shirt tieless; the other detective tall and lean in his navy blue suit, lighter blue tie, and even lighter blue shirt.

"Duffy," said the rotund man, "Ray Duffy."

"Carver," said his partner, "Jerry Carver."

Resisting the impulse to fall into line with "Delafield, Kate Delafield," Kate made no attempt to shake hands with them since they had not offered first; she offered a nod, and her badge and ID.

"You come highly recommended, Detective," said Carver, waving off the ID.

"Especially by Lieutenant Bodwin," said Duffy.

A seed of regard for these two fellow detectives took root. They had assumed nothing, had run a check on her. "Please call me Kate," she said. "And do sit down. Why don't I order us up a couple of pots of coffee."

Uttering simultaneous thanks, the detectives made themselves comfortable at the same small table near the window overlooking the street where Kate had been waiting for them. Where she had watched all the police vehicle activity, the rain-spattered pavement illuminated by strobe-like flashes from the patrol cars' light bars.

"We go by Carver and Duffy," Duffy said, taking out a small tape recorder along with his notebook. "D.C.'s homicide comedy team."

"Right." She could not summon up a smile.

After a few other obvious attempts at ice-breaking from the detectives, including the mention of a mutual acquaintance in San Diego whom she knew through the California Homicide Investigators Association, the room service attendant, escorted by a uniformed officer, arrived with two pots of coffee. As the three detectives filled their cups, Kate reflected that while this might be a far different city from Los Angeles, with different policing problems and logistics, and with police officers who wore different uniforms and bore slightly different titles, they were all cops, blooded and bonded by common battle experience like any Marine Corps platoon. Duffy and Carver already seemed interchangeable with other detectives she had worked with during her police career in Los Angeles, detectives good, bad, or indifferent.

Duffy added five cubes of sugar to his coffee; Carver switched on the tape recorder.

Sipping her coffee, Kate told her story, leaving out only the details of her illicit entry into the bathroom and what she had seen under Allan Gerlock's hand.

"So you have personal history with the deceased," Duffy said, pouring more coffee all around and dumping five more sugar cubes into his own.

"Actually, no. Other people here do. I never met him."

"Is that a fact," Carver said, looking skeptical.

"It's a fact. I can tell you that he was very well liked."

"Not by someone. But you have history with other people here, correct?"

"Vietnam history," Kate said. "I'm friends with a number of people here. Through intermittent correspondence—occasional letters, Christmas cards. I haven't seen any of these people for twenty-five years, I've never met any of their spouses."

Duffy looked confused. "But you still consider them all friends."

"Yes."

"Without even a phone call among you?"

"We never talked."

"Any particular reason you kept your, ah, relationship with them so limited?"

Kate stirred uncomfortably, aware of the tape recorder, aware that any detective would read meaning into her body shift. "We were all in Vietnam together, and we were friends, yes. But Vietnam was a year some of us didn't want to dwell on, and seeing or talking to one another would have . . ." She shrugged. "But some of us began to connect with other vets and for them it was great, they've been gung ho for all of us who served together to reconnect. I wasn't ready for it." She could still feel her sense of betrayal, as if companions on a desert island had paddled away on a raft during the night, forsaking her.

Duffy's nod was sympathetic. "I can understand that. Friends of mine who were there, they're still pretty damn bitter. Myself, I caught a lucky number in the draft." Beneath his faintly ridiculous monklike ring of dark brown hair his grayish eyes were shrewd. But his fatherly, trust-me manner would elicit confidence. And confidences. He had the makings of a good detective.

"My best friend in high school bought it over there," Carver said, his dark eyes meeting hers but focused on a distance of hard memory. "I stayed in college to keep myself the hell out of that shit. Looks like it's caught up with you vets all over again."

Kate nodded in reply. No fatherly act for the saturnine, intimidating Carver. Which made him a good foil for Duffy.

"You said before that you weren't ready to reconnect with the people you served with," Carver said, almost idly. "So how come you're here now?"

She looked at him with growing respect. She might belong to the fraternal order of police, but even if Janet Reno vouched for her she was obviously a suspect to these two particular cops until facts proved otherwise. "An FBI seminar," she answered. "On profiling."

"FBI bullshit," Carver muttered, then scowled at the tape recorder as though he had forgotten about it.

"I didn't get all that much out of it either," Kate commented, and won a hint of a smile from Carver. She went on, "The reunion was a coincidence, scheduled at the same time. I got roped into it."

"By whom?"

"By Melanie Shaw and Aimee Grant," Kate said. "Aimee accompanied me here. I'm not sure where she is and I hope she's being well taken care of." These two men, each wearing a wedding ring, could make of this what they wished. She only cared that they understood that she wanted a special courtesy extended.

But they did not so much as exchange a glance. "She's being looked after," Duffy said. "Jill Manners filled us in on the shooting yesterday." He consulted his notebook. "One of the people with you when you discovered the body, Bernadette O'Rourke Murphy, asked if she could stay downstairs with Miss Grant, and we told her to go right ahead."

"Thank you," Kate said. "I appreciate it."

Duffy switched off the recorder and said, "You made one hell of a good impression on Jill."

Turning off the tape seemed odd, and Duffy's personal comment tangential, until it occurred to her that Duffy might be suggesting off the record that Jill Manners was a lesbian. She chose to reply only with a nod.

"We've got officers, including Jill, questioning all the people at the reunion," Duffy said.

Carver poured more coffee for everyone and switched the recorder back on. "The two events, the shooting and this death, you think they're connected?"

"I don't know," Kate said. But every instinct shouted that they were. "Time of death has to be sometime between when he checked in and before the party started."

"Welcome to Washington, D.C., Mr. Holmes," Duffy said, writing in his notebook for the first time.

"Do tell," Carver said, hunching over to cross his arms on the table, staring at her out of eyes that were like shards of black ice.

Kate enumerated her points on her fingers. "He'd showered—there was every sign of it in the bathroom. He had shaving cream on his face. But no smell of damp or soap or shaving lotion when David Olson and I found the body." She did not mention his warm body temperature when she touched him, but summarized, "He'd come here for the reunion, he was getting ready for it, it began at six o'clock. His uniform was laid out on the bed, he was in the bathroom in a state of partial undress when he was killed—"

"Who told you he was a murder?" Carver demanded.

She needed to tread carefully. "I didn't see any hesitation wounds like you often do on suicides. It didn't seem logical you'd cut your own throat in mid-shave with something other than the razor you're using. I didn't see another weapon, but maybe he fell on it."

"Carver, don't crap around," Duffy said. "He's a murder."

Kate nodded to him and continued. "The killer has to be someone he knew. And trusted. If he wasn't shirtless when he answered the door, he was comfortable enough with his killer to be partly undressed and shaving while the killer was in the bathroom with him."

"No sign of a struggle," Carver conceded. "Just his death throes, and he went pretty fast."

"Right," Kate said somberly. She concluded: "Here's a man who's looking in the mirror and shaving, with his killer in the bathroom with him. Yet he's taken by surprise—and Allan Gerlock had superb military training, even if it was a long time ago. He looked to me to still be in very good physical shape." She said, anguished by the thought, "He would know right away his wound was fatal."

"You took a good long look at the scene," Carver said casually.

"I've been at a lot of scenes," Kate told him. "Twelve years' worth."

Duffy said with a trace of a smile, "D.C. is not L.A."

Unsure of how to interpret his remark, but fully aware that no homicide detective would countenance any encroachment on his or her turf, Kate said, "This case is all yours and you're welcome to it."

"You betcha," Carver said. "The desk clerk said you were down there asking him questions about the shooting yesterday."

"That was different, Carver, and you know it. Either one of you get yourself shot at, you'd do the same thing." She added, "I want no part of your investigation, don't think for a moment I do." In emphasis, she stared at Carver, then at Duffy.

Carver, swirling coffee around in his cup, held her gaze. "Then we understand each other."

Duffy continued to write in his notebook. He said, "Given the circumstances, Kate, it could be a man or a woman in that bathroom with him. Any idea who might do this guy?''

"Not the remotest," Kate said.

"What about the people here—anybody capable of this?"

She answered with a shrug, hoping they would interpret it as a further demonstration of uninterest instead of the only possible response to his ridiculous question.

As in every other homicide case, virtually everyone was capable. And the group attending the reunion was more capable than most. Marines were trained under the most grueling conditions on America's military toughest proving ground to handle weapons—and themselves—in the most effective methods of combat, to be thoroughly committed killers in defense of their country. Even Rachel and Bernie and Melanie had received rudimentary training in weaponry and self-defense in a war zone.

Duffy refined his question: "Anybody have anything against him?"

"Not to my knowledge. Back then I heard one story after another about him and they were all pretty affectionate.''

"Remember any of them?"

She shook her head. "It's been so many years . . .''

"But you had animosities back then?"

"Actually, not many," Kate mused, reflecting over her answer. "A wartime situation, you tend to band together pretty tightly as comrades, you tend to overlook your differences.''

Duffy nodded. "How about now? Anybody act strange tonight?"

Kate smiled thinly. "I wouldn't know."

Carver said, "This reunion. The Marines here, you all in the same unit in Vietnam?"

"No. We're not even all Marines. The other women are mostly Army and Navy nurses and Red Cross. Plus, we're a mixture of officers, NCOs, and enlisted."

"So all you have in common is you hung out together over there," Carver said, looking at her with sharpened interest.

"Right," Kate said.

"I take it most of you are officers?"

"As I said, we're a mixture."

Carver said, "From what I understand, fraternization is a little unusual, isn't it?"

"Nonexistent, in peacetime. A wartime situation, rules get bent, things get a lot more informal."

A lot more, and in many ways. If she hadn't gone to Vietnam, she'd have spent her time in the Corps struggling to turn herself into their standard of comportment, trying to make her hopelessly unfeminine body meet the Marine Corps definition of "conservative but feminine" in a uniform jacket, skirt, and pumps, with lipstick that matched the scarlet braid on her uniform hat.

Duffy flipped back to a page in his notebook. "Tell me if these letters mean anything to you: C, A, and either F or P."

Expecting the question, Kate said, "We served with a man named Charles A. Pearson. He went by his initials, we all called him Cap. He's an MIA."

"You gotta be fucking kidding," Duffy uttered, staring at her.

"You sure about that?" Carver demanded.

"He's an MIA," Kate repeated. "I'm sure of it. Missing and unaccounted for. Why do you ask?" she inquired, knowing they would find it strange if she did not question them.

Writing in his notebook, Duffy said easily, "We saw a reference to those letters in the victim's hotel room."

So Carver and Duffy had succumbed to the same curiosity that had led her into the bathroom to Allan's body. They too had not waited for a coroner to investigate what was under Allan's protective hand; the crime lab van had arrived, but no one from the coroner's office, and she had been watching.

Duffy refilled his cup with more coffee and sugar cubes. Sitting comfortably back in his chair, he said, "We understand it's hearsay, but tell us what you know about the victim."

She shrugged. What she could relate about Allan Gerlock would take Duffy through two sips of his freshly concocted syrup.

"He was rotated out a few days before I arrived as a butter bar. Meaning I wore the brass bar of a lieutenant and was wet behind the ears," she explained to their puzzled expressions. Odd—the jargon had slipped out as easily as if she were back in-country talking to other Marines. "I left the Corps as a captain. From what I know, Allan was never anything but a second lieutenant. In a wartime situation you have to work at not advancing in rank."

Carver said, "So you're telling us he was basically a screwup."

She nodded. "The sergeants used to call Marines who didn't go along with the program shit-birds. In the world of the military a noncomformist stands out like neon. The Corps reams it out of you in basic training or they get rid of you. I don't know how Allan could have made it through boot camp. Marine Corps officer training is so tough . . . Let me put it this way, other military branches put you through hell to get you in good shape to be a soldier. The Marine Corps orders you to get into top shape before you even report for service. Then they still half-kill you. Ten weeks of boot camp and you're expected to run—not march, but run twelve miles up hills and through streams carrying thirty pounds of gear."

Looking impressed, Duffy asked Kate, "Did you do that?"

Kate smiled. "I had eight weeks of OCS—Officer Candidate School. Lots of marching for good posture, lots of classes about how to be feminine and a soldier. Twenty-one weeks of what they called the basic school to learn more fine points about being a proper woman Marine officer. Then a Supply course—school training in my military occupational specialty so I could be a glorified secretary looking after supplies for the troops. We're talking late sixties, Duffy. Women weren't taken seriously, even by women commanding officers. Precious few of us ever got accepted into the Corps; I'm one of a handful who even got to Vietnam. I happened to be recruited when the Corps was ordered to expand their allotment of females."

"Lucky you," Carver said.

Kate could not tell if he was being sarcastic. Hoping he would not ask why she had joined the Marines, she continued, "Even then women were only about one percent of the Corps."

Duffy asked, "What did Gerlock do that he wasn't promoted in rank?"

"I heard he gave the finger to promotions, extra-pay duty assignments. Spit on the Marine Corps reward system, and the lifers—the career officers—will hate your guts."

Duffy's round face bore a faint smile as if he approved of such sedition.

Kate continued, "Undoubtedly it was the reason his platoon was sent up to the Demilitarized Zone, the best place on earth to get your ass shot off."

"What about after he left the Marines?"

"I have no idea. This is the first reunion he's shown up at."

"How many reunions have there been?"

"Three. They started ten years ago—the fifteenth anniversary of when we all served. There was a twentieth and now this one."

"And this is your first one as well."

"Correct."

"Anybody else attending their first one?"

He was asking good questions, Kate thought. "I really have no idea, because I'm not close to a number of people here. But of the group staying at this hotel, it's the first one for Gabriel Bradford, Rachel Summer, Dr. Martin Goldberg, and Dacey—I'm sorry, I don't know his full name, we always just called him Dacey."

"No problem." Duffy was writing rapidly in his notebook. "We need to do next of kin for Gerlock. Any help you can give us with that?"

Kate shook her head. "Sorry."

"What are your travel plans?"

To get herself and Aimee on the next plane out of here even if she had to handcuff Aimee to her wrist. "Both of us were supposed to see more of the city tomorrow, leave for L.A. on Monday."

Carver switched off the tape recorder. "Your lieutenant said you're cleared to remain here as long as it's useful."

Kate said vehemently, "Look, this is—"

"—our case and we're welcome to it," Carver finished for her.

She looked at him in distaste. The brief smile on his thin face could have been on an embalmed corpse.

"You sure now?" he said in acid sarcasm. "We got over five hundred murders this year, we'd never even notice if you took one."

Like hell you wouldn't, she thought.

"Fact of the matter is, we got a little different situation with this case," Duffy said.

Hooking the heel of her boot over the rung of her chair, she looked away from them, leaning toward the window to inhale head-clearing cold air from the slightly open louvers. She hated being involved here; she did not want a molecule of this investigation beyond giving and signing a statement. As retired ex-partner Ed Taylor once said about a detective in West Valley Division who'd gone around the bend looking into the murder of his aunt, *Priests only go to confession to other priests.* Ed Taylor had been lazy as tree sap, but he was right about this. Anything remotely related to anybody who was in the family part of your life, another cop had to take over—the cop part of you had to back away, for the sake of your sanity. She wanted Aimee and herself out of here, out from under this shapeless shadow that had formed over both of them.

"This is our situation," Duffy said, his gray eyes owlish in his round face. "We'll interview everybody here. But my gut tells me this killing has something to do with you. This killing, those shots through your hotel room door, it's all got to be connected. Who knows that it'll stop here? It could follow any of you right back to where you live."

She conceded this with a gloomy nod.

Duffy continued, "We could have a knife, a gun, bloody clothes on these premises. How do you figure our odds on getting a search warrant?"

"Without probable cause? Less than zero," Kate said.

"Bingo," Carver said. "All these people figure to be out of here tomorrow or Monday. Unless something breaks we've got no basis to hold anybody if they want to leave. Which doesn't mean we won't track them to the Arctic Circle if we get a sniff of anything."

"So we'll talk to all these people," Duffy said, "but we don't know what motive somebody might have. You know them. You served with them."

"I don't know anything about them, I can't find out anything more than you can," Kate stated. "They know I'm a cop. I wouldn't have any better advantage than you."

"This is our case. We'll tell them this is our case and you think we stink and you don't want any part of it," Carver said with his embalming-fluid smile. "The D.C. police against the Marine Corps."

Kate turned back from the window. "Carver, Duffy." She spoke their names softly, but with exasperation. "How do you know I didn't do this?"

"We don't," Carver said.

Kate sighed. "There's one other slight problem. These people are all my friends."

"All of them? Everybody here at this reunion is your friend?"

"Some of them," she amended. "And that's another problem. I hardly know some of the people here. The ones I do know best are all staying here at the Inn. Melanie arranged it that way. Someone else in the hotel could have done this," she argued. "Someone connected with Allan but not with the reunion."

Duffy said, "Olson the desk clerk said he was keeping an eye out after yesterday's shooting. He—"

There was a rhythmic rap of four beats. "Excuse me," Duffy said, and got up to open the door to Sergeant Dix.

"Could I see you a moment," Dix said, his gaze flicking over Kate. Duffy stepped out into the hallway.

"One of those guests who's not a part of the reunion could be your killer," Kate continued doggedly.

"We're gonna check all of them out, see if any of them has any connection with the victim. But—"

Duffy came back into the room, sat down again at the table, attempted without success to wring one more cup from the two coffeepots. With a doleful expres-

sion, he reached into his jacket pocket; Kate could see
the wood-grained handle of a nine-millimeter. He
pulled out a package of mints and after offering them
around without any takers, popped two into his mouth.
This guy had either an insatiable sweet tooth, Kate
thought, or he was a recovering alcoholic trying to
quell his body's craving for sugar. By the puffy,
weather-beaten look of him, she guessed the latter.

"Halverson and Palmer found a hotel laundry bag
in the laundry chute," Duffy said. "Containing a
bloody knife wrapped in a towel." He turned to Kate.
"You're exonerated as a suspect."

Kate said, "I could have shot out my own door, got
back inside before Stafford came out into the hallway."

"You're offering us a confession, Detective Delafield?" Duffy was chuckling.

Carver joined in with a wide smile that utterly
thawed his grim face. "So you and Miss Grant are in
cahoots on this caper. Want to tell us how come?"

Kate was grinning in spite of herself. "You two really
are D.C.'s comedy team."

Duffy was looking at his most recent notes. "The
knife's Bowie-style, Dix told me he recognized it
as . . ." Duffy again consulted his notebook, "a K-Bar."

"Shit," Kate muttered.

Carver, his arm along the back of Duffy's chair, had
been examining her. "I would guess it's maybe Viet-
nam-era Marine Corps issue?"

Kate nodded.

"The detective is signifying yes," Duffy said, and
Kate realized with a shock that she had forgotten all
about the tape recorder.

"We'll need to have you sign a statement," Duffy said.

"Of course," Kate said.

"Tomorrow's fine," Carver said.

Kate looked at him. If there was anything further she could give to them, they wanted her to give it right now.

"Kate," Duffy said, "let's put it this way. All of you at this reunion share a common past, you share common memories. If this is some kind of score being settled, if that's the root of this murder, help us at least by trying to remember what the hell it is."

Kate looked from one detective to the other and thought: *Just exactly what I've spent twenty-five years trying not to do.*

"We know you need to be careful," Carver said. "You and Miss Grant. We know you've been shot at." He looked so fatherly that Kate felt that she had misjudged him, felt dislike thawing.

Duffy consulted his notes. "The reunion people staying here at the Inn—you mentioned Gabriel Bradford, Rachel Summer, Dr. Martin Goldberg, and Dacey. Who else is staying here?"

She heaved a sigh. "There's also Doctor Edward Coleman—"

"Two doctors. Heavy duty," said Duffy.

"They'd be real expert at slitting a throat," Carver said.

"Melanie Shaw. And," Kate concluded unhappily, "Woody Hampton."

"This doesn't put you in the stool pigeon class,"

Carver said. "We could get this information from any-body."

Carver was far more acute than she had given him credit for. She said, "The check-in time for every guest at the Inn, David Olson probably has that info in his piles of computer sheets."

"Probably," said Duffy, writing in his notebook.

Ideas forming around the intricacies of this case in spite of herself, Kate said, "You know, if leads don't develop, it might be an idea—" She broke off.

"What?" said Duffy.

She finished reluctantly, "To get the reunion people together again, see how they interact now, after the murder."

"Could be," said Carver. He smiled at her again and snapped off the tape recorder. "Isn't that how Sher-lock Holmes solved his capers?"

"Hercule Poirot," Duffy said.

"Kate, carry your gun," Carver said. "At all times. Beginning now."

Duffy nodded, and popped two more mints into his mouth.

8

WEARY of pacing the length of the Concord Room, Aimee sank into a chair and picked up a water cracker from a tray containing a wedge of Swiss cheese and a carafe of coffee. She tossed the cracker back onto the tray, glanced at her watch. Exactly fifty-five minutes of waiting in this miserable dining room.

She glanced out at the hallway, but the police officer guarding the lobby had again moved off out of sight. The soft-spoken young man had been courteous, twice offering her the option of being taken to headquarters if she would feel safer or more comfortable there. And the tray had been sent in when it became clear that she would remain in this area of the Inn indefinitely.

Quarantine from the room she shared with Kate told her that either a dead body was in that room, or the room was being searched, or Kate was in there being interviewed, or perhaps all three.

She knew Allan Gerlock was dead. Jill Manners had told her that much, and that Kate had found him. Obviously, there would not be this police presence and all this activity if Allan Gerlock had expired from natural causes.

The dining room held the sour stink of overflowing

ashtrays and the alcoholic fumes from abandoned drinks. Plates of food remained on the tables; the waiters had managed to pick up only some of them before the police had arrived and Sergeant Dix had taken charge of crowd dispersion.

She knew better than anyone the unpredictable vagaries of a murder investigation, that detectives needed to follow whatever trail opened to them before any tracks faded. She had been briefly questioned by a sympathetic Jill Manners who quickly ascertained that Aimee knew nothing about what had happened, beyond the fact that Kate and Bernie had left to check on Allan Gerlock's whereabouts.

Aimee groaned as an eviscerated version of "The City of New Orleans" floated out of the speaker in the ceiling. She felt like a prisoner punished by sensory overload instead of deprivation. But the truth was, waiting in limbo seemed a better prospect than facing Kate in the knowledge that if she'd been willing to accept any of Kate's better judgment, the two of them would be long gone from here and Kate would not be enduring any of this.

She crossed her arms protectively over her chest; it still ached from the wrench of panic when the desk clerk had run into the Concord Room: *"Trouble upstairs! Stay right where you are! The police are coming!"*

He'd made things even worse by racing out of the room before anybody could react and slamming the door behind him. And then that damn fool Woody Hampton—actually trying to kick the door down till Gabe Bradford blocked him off and showed him the door wasn't even locked. But she had been on Woody's

side, had been so sure that the "trouble upstairs" involved Kate, and Kate was injured or even dead and all
because of her, that only hearing police sirens had
kept her from clawing her way through Gabe Bradford
and the door. She had borne the tearing of hysteria
for fifteen long minutes before police officers finally
took charge of the room and its occupants.

The image in her mind during those fifteen minutes
had been the blue-gray marble walls at the National
Law Enforcement Officers Memorial in Judiciary
Square. She had gone there alone on Thursday, past
the statuary grouping of a lion guarding its cubs, had
wandered the two tree-lined, leaf-strewn, polished marble paths, gazing at the nearly fourteen thousand
names inscribed on the low, curving walls, officers
killed in the line of duty, about ninety of them women.
The thought, then, that Kate could be one of those
names . . . The thought, now, that she herself could
have been the cause of Kate's name being there—such
an eventuality would destroy her.

At least she and Kate would finally escape from this
loony bin. However long she had to wait, afterward she
would drive Kate straight to the airport and they would
board any plane to Los Angeles even if it was via
Buenos Aires. The damn Muzak was driving her nuts,
she was stir-crazy, she had nothing to read now that
she'd devoured every particle of print in the lobby
copy of the *Washington Post* . . .

"Hi there, honey."

Aimee almost laughed in relief at the sight of Bernie
sailing through the doorway. This time, in place of her
absurd red cocktail dress, she had donned an absurd

chartreuse sweat suit laced with numerous gold chains. In some inverse way the spectacle restored order to the world. Aimee rushed over to her as if she were a long lost relative—and before Bernie could change her mind and escape.

"Oh, God," Aimee gasped as Bernie took her hands, the simple human touch bringing tears. Then she asked in alarm, "What's going on?"

Bernie hugged her. "Nothing. It's okay, everything's okay, honey, believe me. Ralphie's gone to bed, and I just thought you might like some company."

"Have you seen Kate?"

Bernie shook her head. "But she's okay. Turns out your room's right next to ours. I talked to the cop in the hallway, got it out of him that Katie's in there talking to some detectives."

"What happened? Did you hear anything?"

"Not much. You know about Allan—"

"He's dead, that's all they told me."

"The cop in the hallway says somebody did an O. J. on him. Slashed his throat," she amended as Aimee was struggling to make the connection.

"Oh my God," Aimee said, revolted by Bernie's crudeness. In some obscure way she had assumed the man had been shot, which meant she had also assumed in the same obscure way that this death was connected with yesterday's shooting. It occurred to her that Bernie's attitude toward the loss of a friend was callous. "Did you know Allan Gerlock very well?"

"Just when we served together. This is so bizarre. If he was going to be killed, you'd think it would be over there. But yeah, he was one of our gang. All of us, we thought he was a great guy.''

Bernie, she remembered, had put in her Vietnam service in the very center of heavy combat casualties. Her apparent callousness was probably defensive, formed of the same armor of self-protection that Kate wore. "Who would do this to him?''

"None of *us*,'' Bernie said with assurance. She sat down at the table, poured two cups of coffee, handed one to Aimee. "Here, this'll do you good.''

"Something weird is going on,'' Aimee said, uninterested in drinking the coffee but accepting the cup with a nod of thanks and clasping her hands around its warmth. "Our room being shot out yesterday—''

"Yeah. You think maybe it's all connected?'' Bernie tapped out a cigarette from her pack of Salems, flipped open her Zippo.

"Don't you? What else makes any sense? I should never have made Kate come here, I didn't know what I was doing—''

In mid-effort to light the cigarette, Bernie held the flame of the Zippo a scant inch away. "Wait a minute, back up. What do you mean, you *made* her come here?''

Focusing on the coarse, reddish knuckles on Bernie's hands, Aimee hesitated. She had asked Melanie questions, and once Melanie had determined Aimee's state of ignorance about Kate's year in Vietnam, Melanie had been more closemouthed than Kate. "It was after the earthquake,'' Aimee said, meeting Bernie's eyes in a decision that honesty would be her policy, however the results came down. "I found out about all of you—"

Bernie finished lighting her cigarette, tossed the Zippo onto the table with such a clatter that the lobby police officer looked through the doorway, then withdrew. "Earthquake? You mean the big one in January?"

She nodded. Was there any other? "We were both pretty shook up . . ." To put it mildly. She had not been able to utter a sound when the rumbling and violent shaking started, just clung to Kate waiting for the ceiling and the roof to bury them, knowing they would die horribly. Kate was the one who had made the sounds, strangled, guttural, as she tried to protect Aimee with her own body, just as she had yesterday during the shooting. . . . The earthquake was the first time Aimee had learned that Kate was as capable of fright as she was.

"Both of us moved after that—" Immediately afterward, too sobered to wait. Only by chance had they spent that January night together in Kate's apartment, and the real meaning of living apart had suddenly become transparent—an independence which had always had its price and the price was now unacceptable.

That very day of the quake and its teeth-rattling aftershocks, amid all the frantic checking on the safety of friends and relatives in the stricken city, Kate had made her way to the Nightwood Bar to personally seek news of their lesbian friends. There she had learned about Maggie Schaeffer's cousin who was so traumatized from the earthquake and terrified by its aftershocks that she had immediately fled the city. On

Maggie Schaeffer's advice, in a single phone call Aimee placed to Las Vegas, a below-market deal for the West Hollywood condo on Kings Road had been struck.

But she could not explain all that to this straight woman until she knew from Kate how much she could reveal. What a pain in the ass, always having to decide how much of a lesbian you could be, always having to edit your life for everyone you met.

"Anyway, it was during Kate's move, I saw her uniforms all packed away in a garment bag. She had her dog tags and some other stuff in a special metal box. I knew she'd been in Vietnam, but she never would talk about it much, and I asked her some more questions and she just blew me off, which I thought was a bad thing—"

"Honey, it's not necessarily a bad thing."

"Bernie," Aimee said with heartfelt contrition, "I'm really beginning to understand that."

"Katie's not the only one," Bernie said, pulling at the knuckles of her right hand as if they troubled her. "Even all these years later it's hard for some of us to talk about it. Katie's the kind that would find it hardest of all."

"Even agreeing with that," Aimee said, "I still think she needs to talk about it."

"Hey, I don't disagree with you. At some level we all know that. The awful thing is, you just know if you try to talk about it, you might cry, and once you let go, you might never be able to stop."

Moved by what Bernie had just told her, putting it aside for further digestion, Aimee nodded. "She told me a little about some of you, but not much. Then after we moved, the letter came from Melanie about this reunion. I saw it—I'm sorry but I thought it was a good idea for Kate to reconnect with all of you."

Bernie nodded. "I understand."

"I thought maybe she could reclaim a piece of herself. There seems something of her, I don't know . . . not lacking, but . . ."

Bernie looked at her shrewdly. "She's kept a pretty good piece of herself hidden away, hasn't she."

Aimee chose not to answer that directly. "I know Vietnam was a hard place to be, a hard thing to do, all of you went through hell for no decent reason. She claimed she couldn't commit to any particular reunion date because she's always on call to testify in court, you know, it's hard to plan anything. So when this seminar was set up months ago, I phoned Melanie and we cooked up having the reunion the same weekend as her seminar."

Bernie was chuckling. "Believe me, it's the only reason we agreed to have it at such a stupid time of the year, after Veterans' Day and right before Thanksgiving."

Aimee grinned sheepishly. "I sprang it on her just before we were supposed to come here and she was trapped. She couldn't get out of it."

"All of us were so glad to know she'd be here—it's the reason Gabe and Dacey and Rachel decided to show up too." Exhaling a slow stream of smoke, Bernie slouched in her chair. "You really needed to respect her reasons for not wanting to be here."

"I know that now." But that was the point, Aimee thought. She wanted to know what those reasons were, she wanted to share with Kate that pain—whatever it might be, whatever horrors it might hold.

"Bernie, what was she like over there?"

Her amber eyes curtained with thought, Bernie absently stubbed out her Salem. "What was she like . . . A tall, strong kid. Respected by her staff, even by her colonel. Took responsibility, she had what they called command presence. But still, a shy kid. A very likable kid."

Kid. Kate a kid. Aimee struggled with that. It was hard to imagine Kate as anything but an old soul. "What did she . . . look like?"

Bernie grinned. "Skinny. God, we were all so damn skinny. She was . . . she was just *young.* A fine-looking young woman." Bernie chuckled. "But hell, we were all fine-looking. I have yet to see anybody young who isn't fine-looking."

Aimee found this answer highly unsatisfactory. Bernie called Kate "Katie," the only person, to Aimee's knowledge, to ever do so. What had this "Katie" of twenty-five years ago been like? Had "Katie's" light blue eyes looked different back then? What had her arms looked like, her skin, the set of her mouth? She had seen a few early photos of Kate but wanted Bernie's interpretation of those images. "What kind of person was she?"

"Earnest," Bernie said immediately. "Quiet. Sincere. Overwhelmed, like all of us were, in her own way. She wasn't naive, she knew what was going on around her. More than anything, she was real quiet. Lonely. Got quieter all the time. The men called American women round-eyes. Awful term, they had a lot of awful terms back then. We were scarce as diamonds over there, you know, really stood out. Some of us liked it—Melanie did. I could tolerate it, so could Rachel. Katie just withdrew."

Sighing, Bernie sat up in her chair. "It was hard to be a woman over there, if you know what I mean. All that attention smothered you. Mostly you tried like hell to be invisible. Katie tried harder than most of us."

"Does she seem changed to you today?"

Bernie reflected for several moments, pulling at her knuckles. "She seems really together. But hell, what do I know? I've only got so much to go on. She doesn't seem a *whole* lot different today, but I really wouldn't know."

"Whatever she went through over there that she won't talk about . . . Bernie, I have to ask you—do you know what it's about?"

"Aimee, we all went through hell. The details might be different, but it was all hell. You weren't there, you were a little kid—"

Aimee said heatedly, "Okay, I was six years old when Kate was over there. But I tried to learn about the war, I really did. Kate would never watch *China Beach*, but I did, every episode. I read a lot—"

"*China Beach* was good, up to a point. So was *M*A*S*H*. But you still can't really know about it unless you were there," Bernie said. She shook her head. "Never a war like it, especially for women."

Aimee could not ask the question whose complete answer she was most anxious to know: what had it been like for Kate as a lesbian in the elite corps of America's military? She had asked Kate, of course, and Kate had been her usual unforthcoming self: *"The men all believed women had no business whatsoever in the Marine Corps. If we were there it had to be because we were whores or lesbians. I watched out for myself."*

Carefully, Aimee asked Bernie, "Were Kate and Rachel . . . friends?"

"We were all friends. That's why we're here now."

"Were they . . . were any of you . . . especially close?"

"You mean did we have cliques? Oh, sure. Doesn't any group?"

Bernie's answer had been given casually. Too casually, to Aimee's observation. It didn't take a professional detective to notice Bernie take refuge in picking up her extinguished cigarette, examining it, then stubbing it out again.

Aimee approached from another angle. "I spent a lot of time the past few days with Melanie," she said. She had grated on her nerves with her hyperactivity and penchant for deliberately dyslexic figures of speech, such as twisting Aimee Grant into Gaimee Rant.

"What did *she* tell you about Katie?"

"Not all that much. Melanie used to really party a lot with the guys, and Kate was sometimes on the scene."

"Okay." Bernie lit another cigarette. "What did Melanie tell you about herself?"

Aimee closed her eyes to marshal the bits of information she had gleaned about Melanie. "She comes from a little burg in Virginia, she took some training at Camp Lejeune in North Carolina to be able to go to Vietnam, she was in something called SR . . . ah—"

"SRAO," Bernie supplied. "Supplemental Recreational Activities Overseas." She grinned. "They wore silly powder-blue skirts and white boots, and they put on shows and sing-alongs, they helicoptered into combat areas. The guys called them Doughnut Dollies, chopper chicks, Kool Aid Kids. Great young women, very brave. They did a fantastic job, the men adored them."

"I'll bet they did," Aimee said, remembering scenes in a USO club from *China Beach*. "Melanie married a vet who was totally screwed up. Stayed stoned on marijuana all the time. Knocked her around."

"I married a vet too, Aimee. Stayed with him seven years. Lots of us did that." Bernie shook her head. "Mine was a really good guy, but couldn't hold a job, he was totally fucked up too—"

"Aimee."

Kate stood in the doorway. Leaping to her feet, Aimee realized that she had been so focused on Bernie that she had not seen Kate come to the door, nor did she know how long Kate had been there. But she had heard the relief, the love in Kate's voice.

She rushed over to her. Kate seized her in a fierce embrace.

"I'm sorry, I'm so sorry," Aimee whispered.

"It's okay. Aimee, everything's okay."

Aware that they had an attentive audience, Aimee, in some part of her, justified their fervent embrace with the thought that this was like a greeting at an airport, Bernie and the police officer could chalk it up to the stress of the circumstances.

"Let's get out of here," Aimee said.

"We can't," Kate said.

9

AIMEE sat between Kate and Bernie at the table in the Concord Room. Kate seemed tense, her lips drawn tight; she flexed her shoulders and hunched over to stretch her spine as if in confirmation of Aimee's observation. A momentary gap in Kate's jacket revealed a strap; in a mixture of reassurance and alarm Aimee realized that Kate was carrying her gun.

"Getting old, Katie, the both of us," Bernie commented.

"Too old for this, Bernie." Kate crossed her arms, hands clasping her upper arms, and leaned closer to Bernie, looking into the mascara-lined amber eyes as if seeking some connection with this old friend whose life had gone careening off to only God knew where in the past two decades. "Bernie," Kate said, "what do you know about this . . . thing that's happened?"

Bernie shook her head. "Honey, nothing. I haven't a clue why anybody would do this."

"When was the last time you saw Allan?"

"His RTD," Bernie said simply, as if that explained everything. And it obviously did for Kate, who nodded. "I remember like it was yesterday," Bernie added, and again Kate nodded.

"RTD," Aimee repeated.

"Rotation tour date, when Allan was reassigned." Bernie returned her attention to Kate. "Remember, Katie, Allan rotated out just before you got in."

"Right, I remember hearing about it," Kate said.

Frowning, Kate glanced around the Concord Room as if she had only now become conscious of her surroundings. "Smells like a landfill in here. Let's go up to our room." She added, "The Inn's given us a suite. It's an apology for the shooting yesterday."

The clarification about the why of the suite told Aimee that it was important to Kate how Bernie viewed the status of their accommodations.

Bernie said, "I don't care if it's the presidential suite, I ain't going anywhere I can't smoke."

"Cigars if you like," Kate said before Aimee could open her mouth to say their suite was nonsmoking. Obviously Kate needed to talk to this woman. Fine. Anything to be one step closer to getting Kate and herself out of here.

Kate went into the lobby and spoke briefly to the young police officer; Bernie meandered over to the abandoned bar and rummaged around, helping herself to two unopened bottles of Jack Daniels. A portly uniformed officer Aimee had not seen before came into the dining room and announced in a deep Southern accent, "Be glad to take y'all up to the fourth floor."

The desk clerk, looking acutely unhappy, stood at the reception desk talking on the telephone, index finger poised on a list. After a swift glance at them, he returned to his call. "This is the Inn on Liberty

Square," he intoned. "We're very sorry but due to circumstances beyond our control the Patriot restaurant cannot honor any reservations tonight. We will be open for your dining pleasure tomorrow and will be glad to offer as compensation a free—" Wincing, he hung up, pushed strings of blond hair off his forehead and again consulted his reservations list.

Following the police officer down the fourth floor hallway toward the suite, Aimee noticed Bernie's walk. Even with two bottles of bourbon tucked under an arm, she managed to swing her other arm out in a wide arc as if to make up for the deficiency in displacement caused by her small stature.

Kate unlocked the room door. The officer said, "Wait, please," and preceded them, hand on his weapon. He looked around, checking the bedroom as well; then returned and nodded to Kate.

"I appreciate it," she said.

"No trouble at all," he said, and left.

Kate went into the bedroom, and returned shortly, wearing the royal blue souvenir sweatshirt Aimee had bought for her and carrying her shoulder bag. She's put her gun in the bag, Aimee realized.

Kate called down to the desk. "David, sorry to bother you, is room service still available? . . . Yes, coffee, and lots of it. We figure to be up for a while tonight."

Aimee, arms crossed, gazing out the window at the police vehicles parked all around the Inn, barely smothered a groan.

"Ice, we need ice," Bernie called, thumping the bourbon bottles down on the coffee table.

"You heard that, David? Thank you, I appreciate it."

Sitting down at the table in front of the window, Kate placed her shoulder bag at her feet and then met Aimee's eyes in unmistakable communication.

Aimee looked at her pleadingly. The only time she had ever seen Kate performing her job was during their very first meeting, when Kate had interviewed her about a death that had occurred in her aunt's apartment building. She probably would never have so clear an opportunity to see Kate at work—or to peer into the shrouded Kate that she hungered to see.

Kate glanced at Bernie, who was seating herself across from Kate, then back at Aimee, her message plain: I need my conversation to be uninhibited by your presence.

Dejectedly, Aimee said, "Guess I'll go in and lie down for a while."

"Do you good," Bernie said, nodding. "Take a slug of bourbon with you."

"No thanks. See you later."

Aimee went into the bedroom and closed the door. Having spent a night in the suite, she knew its acoustics and that she would hear no more than a low murmur from the living room. The housekeeper had been in; the bedspread was turned down. Kicking off her shoes, she lay on the bed, uncaring of her clothes and thinking disconsolately that she would watch television for a while. She reached for the remote control.

"Aimee can't hear us in there with the door closed."

Kate's voice, coming in faintly through the bedroom window. The housekeeper—it must have been the housekeeper—had opened the side louvers of this window and the one in the living room to allow fresh air into the suite.

Aimee slid over to the side of the bed nearest to the window. Conversation from the suite's other room would be inaudible if Kate or Bernie moved away from the table or if the rain increased, but for now she could hear.

Kate thanked David Olson for the tray loaded with coffeepots, ice bucket, cups and glasses, and touched his arm in comfort; his face was wan, his hands quivered slightly.

Sitting down with Bernie, she said, "Aimee can't hear us in there with the door closed."

She served herself coffee, Bernie waving away the offer. Bernie opened one of the bottles of Jack Daniels. "Take a slug in that coffee. Do you good, Katie."

"Maybe later."

"What, you on duty or something?"

"Not hardly. Booze will make me feel . . ." She hesitated.

"Worse about Allan," Bernie finished for her.

"Yes. I heard so much about him I always felt as if I knew him." Not to mention her own private reasons for regretting his death. Plus, she did need to keep her head clear.

Bernie tossed several ice cubes into a glass and filled it with bourbon, Kate casting a lingering glance at her as she did so. This flamboyant woman in her circus-costume sweat suit and chains seemed a poor impostor for the driven, obsessively ordered woman Kate had known so many years ago. Although Bernie drank hard back then too. They all had, back then.

Bernie took a delicate sip and set the glass firmly back on the table as if that would be the extent of her interest in it. She said, "Aimee seems like a very nice young woman."

"She is," Kate said with a smile. "Smart. Too smart sometimes."

"Pretty, like a movie star. A gorgeous girl."

"She is," Kate said cautiously.

"I must say I wasn't surprised when Melanie told me about the two of you."

Kate sipped her coffee, a prickling between her shoulders from the spotlight focused on this cloaked part of herself. "No?"

"I sort of thought—but you know, you never can tell, you might of found a guy and—"

"I did have a guy," Kate said.

"Well, Katie, we all knew what that was about."

She was surprised—and then annoyed that she was surprised. It should no longer be news that something she had thought to be thoroughly obscured could be transparent to other people. She looked into the life-pounded face of this woman she had not seen in twenty-five years and asked softly, "What the hell happened to you after Nam, Bernie?"

"Tried like hell to find it again, Katie." Bernie's voice was husky. Her hand moved toward the glass of bourbon, circled and squeezed it fiercely. "Couldn't find anything like it. Job after job, man after man, couldn't find any man that lived up to the boys I knew over there, couldn't find the A-number-one team like we had over there, the way all of us came through hell together. Couldn't find the all-out, damn the torpedoes *caring* we gave those guys . . ."

Kate said softly, "*You* gave those guys."

"You too, Katie. We were all in it."

Not like Bernie was, Bernie and Rachel. Her own wartime contributions weren't even on the same planet with those two—not to mention her male Marine comrades, or even Melanie, for that matter. Her profession today was filled with stress, and with the camaraderie and personal loyalties of those who worked at danger's edge, but it was still a pale version of wartime. She wouldn't argue the point. "So you ended up going back to them. Back to a vets' hospital."

"Yeah. It's no way like it was over there, though. I tell you this, Katie—if they're amputees odds are they got it when we were there or before, during Tet. If they're wasted, it was the seventies with the war a goner and everybody on drugs so they wouldn't think about having their balls blown off for no reason on God's green earth." Bernie lit a cigarette, glanced around for an ashtray, slid the saucer from under one of the coffee cups.

Kate said to her, "Bernie, no matter when anybody was there it was bad."

"Tell me the truth, Katie. How you doing? You doing okay?"

"For a while I was just like you, Bernie—"

There was a sharp, rapid knock at the door.

"Shit. Sit still, I'll get it," Bernie said.

Kate opened the louvers wider, to allow the cigarette

smoke to escape. Rain brushed by a slight wind fell in a steady rhythmic patter.

Melanie marched briskly into the room. She wore the same plunging-neckline sweater as at the reunion, but had exchanged her tight black pants for a loose pair of stonewashed jeans with ladders in the knees so wide that the entire kneecap and part of the shin were exposed.

Kate said, "It's okay for you to be here?"

"That Duffy fellow told me where you guys were," she said.

"They questioned you?"

"Yeah, like I was a criminal. I haven't a clue what they thought I'd know—I haven't seen Allan since Nam. Hey, my old friend Dack Janiels," she said, spotting the bourbon on the table.

Kate shook her head. Melanie and her annoying verbal gymnastics.

Melanie picked up the bourbon and a glass from the tray, not bothering with the ice cubes. "Have a drink," Bernie said ironically.

"So what's going on with all this shit," Melanie said, pouring bourbon. "So who offed Allan?"

"We know as much as you do," Bernie said.

Maybe less, Kate speculated. "So bring us up to date," she said. "They tell you anything?"

"Kate, you being a cop here?" Melanie pulled an armchair close to the table and perched on it cross-legged, knees jutting well through her jeans.

"I'm about three thousand miles out of my jurisdiction," she said, resenting Melanie's bold appropriation of her own personal space. And those imitation-poverty jeans Melanie wore, they were despicable when they were trendy, and they were despicable still.

Melanie tossed back a good quantity of her drink. "That tall detective, the creepy one, he wanted to know if I had an alibi for between the hours of four and six—can you believe that?"

"Sure," Bernie said. "They asked me too, and I don't have one—Ralphie was out getting his shoes shined part of that time."

"So you did it," Melanie said. "How come?"

"I think you did it. You were late getting to the reunion party."

"Oh, please," Melanie said witheringly. "Mostly the creepy one was nosing into when all of us were in Nam. Brought back real sweet memories." The moue twisting her face belied her words.

"Just last night I remembered coming in to Tan Son Nhut," Kate said. "Rain, heat, explosions."

"TSN—no rain when I came in but hot and sticky as hell," Melanie said, her fingers plowing a ragged path through her platinum hair. "I thought the natives were all screaming at me—turned out it was the way they actually talked."

Aware of Melanie's racism, Kate did not smile, nor did Bernie.

"Pretty damn exotic for a girl fresh out of Virginia," Melanie muttered around the Winston she was lighting.

"For one fresh out of St. Louis too," said Bernie. "The first time I saw a Vietnamese woman in the *ao dai*—wow."

Kate smiled, recalling the Vietnamese women in

their signature dress, a tight silk tunic with a high slash up the side, panels in the front and back, worn with loose pants. She had thought the garment—and the mature women who wore it—beautiful.

"Street pajamas," Melanie scoffed.

Bernie said, "You liked the young girls in their American miniskirts better?"

"I didn't like anything. You ever see one of their huts?"

"Sure," said Bernie. "Even in our hooches we lived like royalty compared to the peasants."

Kate nodded, remembering structures hardly larger than a typical American bathroom, walls of crisscrossed bamboo and wide leaves, thatched roofs; inside, earthen floors and usually only a crude wooden table, a few stools, a sleeping platform partitioned off by a loosely woven sheet of bamboo. Yes, she had seen rural Vietnam, its hamlets, its peasants in their conical hats, mostly women and children and old men, determinedly working their fields. Cap had taken her, had tried to show her the country's mystique and culture and beauty amid all the poverty and tragedy.

Melanie said, "The one hut I saw, they kept a water buffalo in it."

"They're valuable," Kate said with effort. She wondered if her face had given away the wincing inside her as the ribbon of time brought back traveling in a Jeep with Cap. Seeing up ahead a pair of shouting, laughing Marine officers in a Jeep chauffeured by Dacey and Will Maloney, the officers riddling a water buffalo with bullets while a Vietnamese family lay prostrate and sobbing in despair. Cap had reported the incident, and, it seemed to her now, had set into motion the whole series of events that had resulted in his reassignment and disappearance.

"I never saw chickens and pigs so scrawny," Melanie said. "Hardly any hair or feathers."

Bernie took a deep swallow of bourbon. "Tapeworms," she said succinctly.

Melanie shrugged. "Nothing in the whole damn country worth fighting over. TSN, that was okay," she conceded, dragging smoke from her cigarette. "Big USO club. But the Red Cross center at Da Nang was great, great PX, USO. Great guys . . ."

"Rats, snakes, monsoons," said Bernie, dropping a conspiratorial wink to Kate.

"Mosquitoes," Kate contributed, picking up on Bernie's hint. "Incoming artillery. My first night in Da Nang I slept under my bed." She had. And occasional nights thereafter. Artillery rounds from surrounding hills had sounded, and felt, as if they were landing right outside her Quonset hut.

"The food," Bernie said. "Horrible mess hall."

"Oh, come on." Melanie flicked cigarette ash into Bernie's makeshift ashtray. "The guys kept all the women in steak and lobster."

"To this day I can't abide either one," Bernie said. "Melanie, why the hell did you go over there?"

Melanie chuckled. "My dad went nuts. He always said how glad he was he couldn't send a son to war."

It wasn't an answer to Bernie's question, Kate thought. But then again, maybe it was.

"How about you," Melanie asked, "how come you went, Bernie?"

"To fight the devil. I believed every fucking thing they told me about communism being the devil incarnate."

"Bernie," Kate said softly, "you loved your country and you wanted to serve."

"I was clueless," Bernie said, and focused on her drink. But Kate had seen a glimmer of tears.

We were all so naive, Kate thought. We truly believed JFK about needing to aspire to something larger than ourselves. Before cynicism became an article of faith.

"I wanted to serve too," Melanie asserted. "I thought all the people criticizing this country were scum. I still do, goddammit. Nobody thought I could go off to war and take on responsibility, but I did. Besides," she added with a giggle, "I thought it would be fun. And it was. It—" She coughed. "It was..." Her voice broke. "It was the greatest goddamn year of my whole goddamn life."

Bernie cast a brief but sympathetic look at Melanie. "And what about you, Katie? How come Vietnam?"

She would not be ensnared in confessional melodrama. "I was a stupid kid, I just went where the action was."

"Bullshit," pronounced Bernie. "Let's get to the better question. How come the Marines?"

Kate poured herself more coffee. "Bernie," she said, "didn't we talk about all this stuff when we were over there? I honestly don't see any more of an answer now than when I went. I didn't have much of any politics then, I don't know that I do to this day—" *Other than being clear on the people who want to control or harm me.* "My dad was Army," she said. "World War Two—"

"Mine too," Melanie said. "I never heard the end of it."

"Me either," Kate said, smiling at her. "My dad fought in Germany, his only brother was Navy, died in the Atlantic, my aunt drove an ambulance in Italy."

Melanie said, "So you joined the Marines and topped everybody."

She was struck silent by the remark. She had always traced her primary motivation back to the recruiting poster she had seen as a child: a Marine in dress blues, the eagle, globe, and anchor on his cap and collar, his stern face symbolizing the strength and the very best of America—loyalty, courage, commitment. She had believed she would find the strongest, most admirable women in the Marine Corps, and she would match her strength to theirs.

After the affair with Julie she hadn't known what to do with her life. Hadn't known what to do about a father with anxious expectations for an ungainly daughter who was all that remained to him after his wife's death. As widow Aunt Agnes had made patently clear on many occasions, Kate was the end of the De-lafield line—the complications of her birth had not only ended all hope for a male Delafield, but had sown the seeds for her mother's early death.

Her father had been so proud of her. Too proud of her and her one singular accomplishment: that she had fulfilled her mother's own impossible dream of being the first woman on either side of the Delafield family to attend college.

Her father's reach in life had been to open a land-scaping business that would take his gift for horticulture beyond the spectacular garden around their modest house. But his grasp had ended at being crew chief of the three sanitary workers in the town of Greenleaf, Michigan. She herself hadn't had any ambitions, beyond mouthing a vague desire to venture into the legal profession, and somehow managing, financially and intellectually, the four daunting years of a college curriculum of courses in law and business administration. Her junior year had brought the realization that she did not have an idea in the world about her real future. In the absence of a definitive goal, military service would be a creditable haven until she found an answer—or perhaps so that she could continue to avoid one.

Melanie's offhand remark was exactly on the mark. When the young Marine Corps recruiter had braved a single visit to the 1960s-hostile University of Michigan campus in his dress uniform, he had been the only recruiter she had talked to. Because Marine Corps Officer Candidate School would raise family military tradition to a higher plane. Because she would be contributing to her country, even if most of her peer group didn't think so. Because becoming a Marine Corps officer would allay the anxiety in her father's eyes, would earn his pride in her one exemplary choice.

And yes, her father had been proud. The look on his face the day she had marched in full dress uniform on parade at Quantico to be commissioned as an officer had made everything almost worth it. Almost.

Bernie said, "Come on, stop the woolgathering, answer the question, Katie."

"Well—"

Another knock on the door.

"What is this, a goddamn boardinghouse?" grumbled Bernie, getting to her feet. "You won't be saved by the bell, Katie."

Dacey walked into the room. "So this is where the action is. Hey, Kate, two detectives, a fat little fellow and a tall guy, they seemed real interested about you and Cap."

10

"THAT'S funny," Melanie said, "they asked me about Cap too."

"And me," Bernie said.

"Any idea why, Kate?" Dacey said.

"No more than you," she said, watching him make his way into the room, noticing his expensive-looking cowboy boots. Could they be alligator? Wasn't that one of the endangered species?

Even though he was not wearing military fatigues, the up-on-the-balls-of-his-feet cautious grace of his walk brought back the dramatic circumstances of her first encounter with him.

She had been in the 95th Evac talking, or rather listening to Bernie, who, learning that a newly arrived boot lieutenant in Supply was a woman, had promptly hauled Kate in to listen to her wrathful complaints about the chronic and criminal shortages of such basics as suction tubes. Kate was sympathetically listening to Bernie's diatribe, taking notes, when Bernie cut herself off, both women hearing what would become for Kate the soundtrack of Vietnam—the resounding eggbeater clatter of approaching helicopters.

"Incoming wounded!" Bernie shouted, already on the run.

As Bernie and assorted other nurses pulling gurneys rushed out to the triage area, Kate uncertainly trailing in their wake, a cluster of dustoffs came floating in from the direction of blue-green Marble Mountain. Dacey was first off the lead chopper before it had fully settled into its landing, emerging in the doorway, M-16 in hand, leaping out to help unload the wounded.

In those early days in Vietnam, he was the first fresh-in-from-the-bush combat Marine she had seen and she stared at him, partly in fascination and partly to avert her eyes from the carnage being hastily pulled off the chopper, Marines on stretchers, their jungle fatigues and makeshift bandages and splints blood-soaked, their stoic silence seeming to echo in her appalled ears despite the whirring helicopter blades and the triage nurses screaming priorities for the various injury trauma levels.

Shooed off by the nurses and medics, Dacey moved away to stand to the side of the frenzied activity, lowering his gun and his pack to the barren earth along with a cartridge belt onto which he had tied extra canteens and grenades. His face was obscured by his helmet and the thick reddish-brown dust whirled up by the choppers, which one by one were taking off to return to the mountain jungles as soon as their cargo of damaged human beings had been deposited; but she could see his slender frame, his green pants banded and streaked with white, torn out at both knees; and she could see his feet. Accustomed to gleaming black polish, she was amazed by his boots: countless abrasions had scraped the leather virtually clean of color. Bandoliers of ammunition crisscrossed his filthy flak

jacket, its bottom section hacked off, the jacket hanging open over his sleeveless green T-shirt which, she
would learn, substituted for the standard issue long-
sleeve shirt unsuited to this torrid heat and humidity.

She had assumed he would climb back onto one of
the dustoffs to return to the field, but as the last one
took off, he picked up his gun and belt and pack and
strode with lithe economy through the settling dust
clouds toward her.

Blondish hair hung out from the sides and back of
his helmet on which was scrawled YOUR FRIENDLY VC
EXTERMINATOR. His nose was mahogany with sunburn;
but above the dark stubble on his face, shaded by the
helmet, his forehead was shockingly white. Bare, string-
ily muscled arms, also tanned to mahogany, were
striped red and white from slashes in various stages of
healing; she would learn that many of these were from
wait-a-minute vines, common to Asia and so named because they tore at whatever they had grappled onto
unless you stopped to remove them. The patch signifying his rank of corporal was fastened to the flap of
his flak jacket, and around his neck hung a rag, too
filthy with dirt and sweat to guess its original hue, and
only one dog tag; she would learn that the other was
in one of his lacerated boots for identification in the
event that his chest was blown apart. He also wore another necklace of what appeared to be dried brown
leaves . . .

His lean body was rock-solid yet fluid in movement,
his blue eyes watchful, hard, alligator-flat. He was
youthful, powerful, a perfectly efficient killing machine, and she stared at him in dread and in passionate

admiration, not for his potential for destruction but for the raw purity of purpose in him.

His eyes glancing off her stare, he pulled up short in front of her in his own amazed scrutiny of the breasts covered by her fatigues. "My God, a round-eye." Then he saw the brass bar on her collar, and snapped to attention with a salute and stammered, "Sorry, ma'am, very sorry, Lieutenant."

"Good luck to you, Corporal," she had told him, returning his salute, and turned to make her way back to her Quonset-hut office, hearing out of the tumult of the triage area Bernie's urgent demand: "Plasma! IV!"

"Got all the luck I need, Lieutenant," Dacey had responded to her back. "I'm in one piece, I'm here in the rear with the beer till I ride the Freedom Bird home."

Home. So where was his home now, with Cap apparently no longer in his picture? She said to him, "Where are you living these days, Dacey?"

"Kentucky," he said, looking around. "So where's your nice young friend?"

"Lying down," Kate said, appreciating that his characterization of Aimee did not contain any of the usual male references to her physical attributes.

"What a bummer of a night," Dacey said, shaking his head. "The guy was so young—still in his forties, for God's sake. Mind if I have a slug of this booze?"

"It's Bernie's," Kate said.

"It's the Inn's," Bernie said, flicking ash into her saucer, not looking at Dacey. Bernie had never liked Dacey. Kate struggled to remember why.

"I guess Puff the Magic Dragon wouldn't be a hot idea with all these cops crawling around," Melanie said, eyeing her purse.

"One right in this room," Dacey said with a quick grin at Kate. He had moved over to the window to watch the street activity.

"Off duty and out of jurisdiction," Kate tossed in for what it was worth. But if Melanie was idiot enough to expose a stash of marijuana, she would frog-march her and her stash out of the room and into Rudy's and Jill's arms.

"Bring weed out, I'll bust your ass if Kate won't," Bernie stated.

"Oh, of course, Mother Superior," Melanie sneered. "Booze is so much more godly than weed."

"I wonder why you don't seem too upset about Allan," Bernie returned in a tone that matched Melanie's.

If Melanie was caught off guard by Bernie's deflection in subject matter, she didn't show it. "You don't either," she retorted.

"He wasn't *my* old flame."

"Mine either, except for two silly minutes." Melanie traced a chip in the blood-red nail polish on her index finger in blank-faced concentration.

"Till he dumped you. Till—"

"Just shut the fuck up." Melanie did not look up, and her voice was completely toneless.

"Come on, Mel," Dacey said, "this is old history—"

"Don't *you* go philosophical on me, Dacey," she said with a cold sideways glance at him. "What do you know? You never even met Allan."

He looked startled by her hostility. "I don't know

why anybody would give a fuck," he said, and lit a cigarette.

"Somebody does," Melanie mused. "Somebody
made Allan fuck off permanently, and the cops are
asking all these questions about Cap."

"The cops can piss up any tree they like," Bernie
said, stubbing her cigarette out in her saucer. "They
can't possibly believe this has anything to do with us—"

"Oh, get real," Melanie snorted. "There's got to be
some reason they're bringing up—"

"A dead man," interjected Dacey.

"Missing," hissed Bernie, taking the word out of
Kate's mouth.

"Missing," Melanie repeated, nodding. "I figure
Kate knows why."

"I haven't the slightest idea what a missing man has
to do with Allan Gerlock's death," she said, and was
greeted by a silence broken only by the gurgle of bourbon being poured into Melanie's glass.

Another knock on the door. With a sigh, Melanie
got up.

"It's Cock Doleman and Sachel Rummer," Melanie
greeted Doc and Rachel. Rachel, rolling her eyes,
brushed by Melanie without saying a word.

Dacey tossed Rachel and Doc a cheerful mock-salute.
"If you show up here, it means the cops haven't arrested you."

"They acted as if they just might," Doc said. "The
one guy was like Joe Friday. Questions from everywhere, especially left field."

Kate grinned; she could understand why Carver had
focused his questions on Doc.

Rachel still wore her military shirt and jeans, but Doc's red pin-striped Philadelphia Phillies baseball jersey hung well off his narrow shoulders and down over jeans baggy in the seat; a battered red baseball cap sat sideways on his head. He looked, Kate thought, as cheerfully ridiculous as he had in his previous costume—he must be going out of his way to look eccentric. Gazing at Rachel, Kate was struck by her evident distress over the events of the evening: Rachel's dark eyes were edged in red and seemed large against the pallor of her face.

Bernie grabbed a few more ice cubes from the bucket, tossed them into her bourbon. "Help yourselves," she invited Doc and Rachel.

"Don't mind if I do," Doc said. Rachel declined with a head shake and an effort at a smile, reaching instead for the coffee carafe.

"Is Maria all right?" Kate asked Doc.

"Sure. I left her on the phone telling her sister in Guatemala what a nightmare place Washington, D.C. is."

All these visitors were rapidly depleting the supply of cups and glasses. And bourbon too, the way Bernie and Melanie and Dacey were tanking it down. But then she wasn't running a bar in here. But could she ever use a good stiff belt of the stuff herself.

Kate got up as Rachel finished pouring herself coffee, offering her a seat at the table.

"Thanks, I like the floor—remember?"

Kate smiled. "I do remember."

"What happened tonight, it brings it all back . . ." Rachel did not finish, but arranged herself near the window, beside the sofa, her back up against the wall, ankles crossed, facing the table where Kate sat with Bernie, Dacey, and Doc. In Nam, whether in Rachel's hooch or in Kate's, Rachel had always preferred to sit on a pillow, her back against the plywood paneling. It struck Kate now that Rachel had been the only non-smoker Kate had known in Vietnam—not for lack of Rachel's trying; she claimed she could not inhale. Quite possibly Rachel had always sat on the floor to escape the noxious fumes produced by all the smokers around her, including Kate herself.

"Your pretty friend," Doc said to Kate, "she's escaped back to Los Angeles?"

"She wishes," Kate said, inclining her head in the direction of the bedroom where, hopefully, Aimee was getting some sleep. She'd check on her later.

"Rachel, what do you know that we don't?" Melanie inquired.

"About Allan? Nobody in the world knows less about Allan than I do."

"Well," Melanie said airily, "he claimed to know a few things about you."

Rachel gazed at Melanie calmly, with infinite weariness. "And on that basis I cut his throat, is that what you're hinting?"

"Why not," Melanie replied. "I'll bet you don't have an alibi."

"Girls, girls," Dacey said, spreading his hands.

"Where, where?" Bernie cast looks all over the room, including at the ceiling. "I don't see any girls in here."

"For God's—look, give me a break," Dacey said, "I didn't mean—"

Another knock on the door. "Get that, would you, Doc?" Kate said, wondering about Melanie's comment, and Rachel's reaction, and thinking that Carver and Duffy were sending everyone to this room with deliberate purpose and without any concern about keeping witnesses separated, perhaps because none of them had actually witnessed anything. Also, it was an efficient way to keep tabs on everyone's whereabouts. In any event, she was being forced to concede that the case detectives were correct in their assessment of this murder: its solution lay in investigating the past, not the present.

Gabe came in; Kate was glad to see him. Like Rachel he too had not changed out of his military fatigues, including his cap. After a swift, assessing look around the room, he somberly poured himself a glass of water from the suite's wet bar and made his way over toward the table and lounged against the wall.

Kate remembered Rachel talking about Gabe and Allan Gerlock, that they were two young men dissimilar in background and personality who had circled each other in curious fascination, their jagged personality patterns somehow fitting together; and they sometimes hung out together. Dustoff pilot Will Maloney, who, Kate had learned earlier tonight, was now dead, had also been a shit-bird with a rebellious swagger equal to Allan's, so counter-culture to the discipline and tradition of the Marine Corps that the lifers had lumped both of them in with the insolent clique of young black-power soldiers and dismissed them all as "niggers."

Allan's reassignment to the DMZ had undoubtedly been payback time. Conformist Marine Gabe Bradford had never fit into the shit-bird mold—his relationship with Allan had been on an altogether different plane. . . . Had Allan and Gabe kept in touch? Was there something between the two of them that the reticent Gabe was holding secret?

Odd—of the triumvirate of Gabe, Will Maloney, and Allan Gerlock, two of the three were dead. And Cap . . . what about Cap?

Doc too got himself some water, asking, "Anybody else get asked questions about Cap?"

"I got peppered with questions about him, about everything," Gabe said. "What I did all day today, where I was yesterday when Kate's room got shot up."

"They asked me that stuff too," Doc said, "I don't get it." He turned his attention to Kate. "They were real interested in you, Kate, you and Cap. You a suspect?" His grin conveyed the absurdity of such an idea.

She nodded, adding, "We're all suspects."

Doc waved a hand in dismissal. "Seriously. Why do they care about that lovely boy who's been missing all these years?"

Dacey said, "If Cap were alive they'd have found him by now."

"I don't agree," Kate said tersely.

"I'm sorry, Kate," Dacey said to her. "Truly sorry for what I just said. From everything I heard about him, he was a great guy."

"Forget it," Kate said. Just because she had never come to definitive terms with Cap's disappearance, she could hardly blame anyone for accepting that Cap was dead.

"I had the oddest feeling tonight," Rachel said, balancing her coffee cup on her thigh. "Like Cap would come walking in the door of the Concord Room and say, 'Didn't I play a good one on all of you all these years.' "

"Jesus," whispered Melanie, her eyes squeezed shut.

"Rachel, I had the exact same wish," Gabe said softly. He was leaning against the wall, glass of water in one hand, cigarette in the other.

"Never, I've never given Cap up for dead," Doc declared.

Pummeled by emotion, Kate looked at all of them in amazement. If only Cap could hear this, see this affection for him undimmed by the years. It was as if the people in this room were a family of sorts which had no more lost hope for its own MIA than had the families of those more than sixteen hundred unaccounted for to this very day.

"I just wish I could have seen Allan," Doc said, peering into his glass of bourbon as if he sought Allan Gerlock's image in it. "I wanted him to know about my life these days."

Kate watched him. Was Doc trying to establish that he had not seen Allan before his murder?

"I told him, Doc," Melanie said, and picked up her bourbon.

"You did?" Doc looked at her in clear annoyance. "Melanie, you could have let me—well, it's all pretty damn academic, isn't it." He turned his attention to Kate. "I take it you didn't think much of the news."

Kate was bewildered. "What are you talking about?"

Doc said to Melanie, "You told Allan but not Kate?"

Melanie sighed, then spoke with the exaggerated patience of someone addressing a fool. "Doc, I didn't talk directly with Kate about the reunion. Only to Kate's friend, Aimee."

"I see," Doc said. "Kate, you and Allan were out of the loop way too long. I'm not practicing medicine anymore."

"So we should be calling Doc ex-Doc," Dacey joked.

Kate's attention was fully on Doc. "You *what?*"

"I still use my skills. I'm a glorified, very well-paid technical writer. I take research results and verification data, synthesize it all into an intelligible format and add a synopsis and index."

Kate could not believe her ears. Rachel was looking at her with a wry smile, as if she understood Kate's reaction perfectly. And of course Rachel would. In Vietnam she and Rachel had bestowed the nickname of Ben Casey on Doc because he so closely resembled the bristling, driven, dedicated hero of the old television series. Kate could not have been more astounded had he gone into witchcraft.

"Doc, why didn't you tell me this before?"

"I was saving it as a surprise, for both you and Allan."

Saving it? A surprise? His explanation made no sense. "I can't believe it," she uttered.

"Believe it." Bernie bit the words off. "Doc's thrown his talent in the toilet."

"Bernie would think so," Doc said imperturbably, touching the bill of his baseball cap as if to insure that

it sat correctly sideways on his head. "Bernie never realized she was a better doctor than I was."

Kate shook her head as if to clear cobwebs from her
memory. The Doctor Edward Coleman she knew in
Vietnam had made medicine a calling. That confident
stride through the wards on his daily rounds of the
boys in those hospital beds—and with their military
accouterments removed and fear in their eyes they had
reverted to being boys—that serene assurance of his
that they would recover and be celebrated heroes in
the eyes of their country, and all of it accomplished
with the majestic omnipotence of a visiting general.
The young Marines, however badly wounded they
might be, had responded at least briefly to the bracing
tonic of his confidence. She could give her own personal testimony. Afflicted by FUO—fever of unknown
origin—a typical malady in Vietnam, but with deadly
potential in her case, she had been hospitalized until
her temperature came down from 105 degrees, and he
had been her doctor. And Rachel . . . Rachel had been
her nurse . . .

Kate found herself planted firmly in Bernie's corner
in condemning Doc. This man of rare gifts had thrown
all of them away and turned himself into a cartoon. It
made no sense. She demanded heedlessly, "Doc, how
could you do this?"

He looked at her, his blue-green eyes glistening behind the tiny lenses of his glasses. "What everyone
thought they saw in Nam was a sham. I committed
crimes against humanity."

"What stupid utter fucking bullshit," muttered Bernie.

"Allan Gerlock, that's what I call a crime against humanity," Rachel said, nodding at Bernie. "Among other things . . ."

"Doc, I think maybe somebody committed a crime against your head," said Gabe.

"To each his own," Melanie said. "Doc doesn't have to live his life the way we happen to think he should."

"Thank you, my dear," Doc said, lifting his baseball cap to her. "I couldn't have stated it better."

Another knock at the door. Gabe detached himself from his leaning position against the wall to answer it.

Woody stepped in front of Martin and preceded him into the room. With an inclusive wave at the group, he addressed Kate: "The tall dude and the fat one, they want to see you, Kate. They said to get your tail down to the Concord Room right now."

Martin stopped in the doorway and surveyed the group, eyeing Doc with a snort and a shake of his head, then made his way into the suite. "What a night," he groaned. "With the level of police competence in this town, they'll arrest us all, lose the paperwork, we'll rot in jail for the rest of our days."

He picked up the second bottle of Jack Daniels. "Just what the doctor ordered."

"Gee, I'm sorry to see you so upset over Allan's death," Melanie said.

"Kate," Woody said, "I thought the tall dude was gonna shit his pants about you and Cap. You did tell them you were engaged to Cap, didn't you?"

11

"IT'S of no importance at all," Kate told Carver.

She, Carver, and Duffy sat together in the Concord Room, at the same table where she had earlier found Aimee and Bernie. For this interview there was no tape recorder. Duffy was again drinking coffee, sitting calmly back in his chair, cup and saucer in hand; Carver leaned toward Kate in grim ferocity.

His lips hardly moved as he spoke: "Give me at least one good reason, Detective Delafield, why we should believe that your engagement to Charles A. Pearson has no importance to this case."

She could imagine that many suspects had been impaled on Carver's feral stare, especially with Duffy's body English communicating that he had surrendered full rein to his partner. "I can give you at least three," she answered, and ticked them off on her fingers. "First and foremost, it was twenty-five years ago, and over with back then. Second, Cap is an MIA. Third, when we talked before all you said was that you'd found a reference to Cap in Allan's room—why would I attach any significance to that?"

"Detective," Carver said, his tone no less hostile, "we have no way of telling what you were doing in that room—"

"I gave you my statement."

"—and frankly, it's pretty clear you have no intention of coming clean with us."

Kate held his stare and did not reply.

In the silence, Duffy offered, "Well, Kate's a detective."

The smile that split Carver's face was so brilliant that Kate thought of a coconut cracking open to reveal its dazzling white contents. "You do keep your own counsel, Detective," Carver said.

As if you don't, she thought.

"I admire cops like that," he said.

"We all do it," she said neutrally.

Duffy leaned forward, put his elbows on the table, and looked at her with cool gray eyes, all evidence of congeniality gone. "Tell us about Cap Pearson."

Hoping to narrow their area of interest, Kate temporized. "What do you want to know?"

"Detective," Carver said with a chastising head shake, "answer the question."

"I met him right after I was in-country," Kate began, trying to dredge up memory and to arrange her thoughts at the same time. "Cap arrived two days after I did. He was the only junior officer I'd met up to that point who hadn't been sent right to the field. Infantry-trained officers normally see action the first part of their tour, then rotate to the rear. But Cap was assigned to S-Five."

She waved off Duffy's offer of coffee; she'd had so much to drink she felt waterlogged. "S-Five was a good-will program, a small unit of Marines dealing directly with Vietnamese in the countryside. Building roads,

digging wells, minor medical care, things like that."
She said with a half-smile, "It was called the Civic Action Program. We used to tease Cap that he'd been assigned to the program because it had the same initials he did. But he was perfect for it—he was the quintessential all-American boy."

"That's how Rachel Summer described him. Melanie Shaw says he was . . ." Duffy paused, as if to quote her, "a fine-looking young man with great charisma and great character."

"Blond, blue eyes, rugged, handsome," Kate enumerated, "masculine, personable, principled—"

Duffy again interrupted. "Everything going for him, is what Dacey says."

"Let her talk, Duffy," Carver said.

"He did," she said to Duffy. "Self-made—"

"How so?" Carver asked, and Duffy grinned at his partner's immediate contradiction of his own order.

"Put himself all the way through college on scholarships." If college was an experience she and Cap shared in common, she hadn't had nearly enough smarts for scholarships; she'd worked her tail off at waitressing jobs, not to mention in the classroom and lecture halls.

"So you were engaged to this male paragon," Carver reminded her. "An event you claim has no importance."

Kate said awkwardly, "It was something that seemed a good idea at the time."

"Gabriel Bradford told us that Cap was gay and everybody knew it," Duffy said, and was rewarded by a fiery glare from his partner.

"So," Carver said in a tone of utter disgust, shaking his head at his partner, "was he?"

Grateful to Duffy, who did not look repentant in the slightest for having breached good questioning technique by answering a question pointed straight at her heart, she still hesitated. She had had to reveal such information about herself, but never had she identified anyone as gay to someone outside the circle of the gay people she knew, even if a straight person claimed inside knowledge. Still—what difference did it make now? Cap was either perfectly hidden, or perfectly dead.

"Yes, he was gay," she said.

"That took a while," Carver observed.

"It isn't something I usually do," Kate said.

"Aren't these different times?" Duffy said.

"Not especially." Was he baiting her? He had to know that police in general were as homophobic as the military organizations they resembled. "Revealing is exposing," she said. "Life is tough enough."

Duffy said, "One day a year the gays go parading around saying how proud they are, the rest of the time they hide their heads."

"I'm not hiding my head," Kate said evenly.

"Duffy, just fucking stuff it," Carver said. He turned back to Kate. "So, if everybody over there knew he was gay, why wasn't he investigated? Kicked out?"

"I can't verify that everybody knew it," Kate said. Although it looked to her today as if everyone had. "But I can tell you that the military kicks gays out only in peacetime, not wartime." She remembered reading in a magazine article that Randy Shilts' book, *Conduct*

Unbecoming, claimed that the veranda of the officers' club in Da Nang had been prime gay cruising territory—a fact not evident to her while she was there. The book also claimed that General Westmoreland had been surrounded by a staff of gay men. Maybe so, but women were kicked out anytime and all the time. As she discovered when she returned to the World and witnessed the military careers of women all around her picked off for destruction with the seeming randomness of target practice. Her rank and her service in a combat arena had distanced her from most other women Marines, had served as a wall of protection—and isolation.

Naive could have been her middle name, she thought angrily. Naive hyphenated with stupid. Even at the age of twenty she had known better than to walk into anything with her eyes shut, especially an organization to which she had committed four years of her life. She hadn't had the slightest inkling that in the eyes of all branches of the military, and especially the Marine Corps, she would be held in equal contempt with gay men—and considered far more expendable, the Marine Corps expelling for sexual orientation seven times more of its tiny component of women than it did men. She had had to find out the hard way that any woman not in the nurturing profession of nurse was an interloper in their male preserve—either a whore who had joined the Marines in conscious or unconscious search of a real man to screw her, or a queer imitation of a man, with no rational reason or right to think she belonged on an equal footing with real men.

At least she had been a quick study, learning to skate

carefully and discreetly within this cesspool, with the advantage over other women Marines of having an officer's rank to afford some protection. But she had to live and work with male officers of equal or greater rank, she had to endure with the best grace and humor she could muster their endless overtures, teasing, innuendo, covert insults, harassment.

Cap Pearson, albeit amusing and charismatic, had been one more nuisance adding to the mind-numbing routine of her clerical duties, and she fended off his flirtation with her usual one-size-fits-all bantering refusal: "You're just not my type, but if you were . . ." When he learned that she could no more circumvent the cumbersome and exhausting mandates of the military's paperwork network than he could, his flirtation became perfunctory and she had discovered with a degree of chagrin that he had exerted his charms mostly to benefit his severely underfunded and undermanned Civil Action Program.

Carver asked ironically, "So how well did you know your fiancé?"

"Very well. I admired him tremendously, we spent a lot of time together."

He continued to hang around her desk because hers was a ready and commiserating ear for his frustrations. Then one day: "Why don't you come out with me and Bernie to one of the villages?" And she had gone, had distributed a few clothes and some packets of food while Bernie treated reed-slender children for skin infections and parasites. And that was the first time Kate had begun to see beyond the wraith-like hooch girl who came into her quarters and for three dollars a week cleaned her room and washed her clothes. To see beyond the contempt for the Vietnamese people displayed by Marine commanders whose mission it was to defend them. She had begun to see the quiet, dignified faces of Vietnamese women with eyes haunted by tragedies beyond her imagination. To see into a centuries-old culture and belief system of a people caught between two warring ideologies irrelevant to their daily lives. Thanks to Cap.

She told Carver and Duffy, "He was, in his own way, a hero."

As often as she could, sometimes with Rachel or Bernie, she had ridden as a volunteer in the one rattletrap of a Jeep assigned to S-Five, venturing into small hamlets in-country. She had attended briefings to hear Cap plead his case, before the stonily indifferent Marine Corps brass, that the American military had an obligation to bring to an ancient people any tools they could use to ease their harsh lives, to help them carve out some kind of an existence during a conflict tearing their country, their livelihood, their families, their lives, their very culture apart.

Kate said, "Colonel Daley told me Cap's project turned three entire villages into allies who actually reported VC activity to us." She asked rhetorically, "Don't you think that's more valuable than winning a hill only to have to retake it a few weeks later? But they pulled the plug on Cap's project."

Duffy shook his head. "I can guess why."

"Our own commanders claimed we were throwing away resources on a cowardly, ungrateful people. The Saigon regime didn't want anything distributed directly to the people that they couldn't get their hands on first."

It was not from antiwar protests at home—she would not fully experience those until later—but from Cap that she learned the truth about this war, about villagers who had turned to the Vietcong in despair over the hopelessly corrupt government in Saigon, about North Vietnamese Army soldiers capable of cutting breasts and hands off villagers to compel their allegiance to Hanoi, about brutal American "defenders" whose My Lai-type atrocities occurred both before and after the American public learned of them.

"You confirm that the man was gay," Duffy said. "How did you know?"

"Because of what happened a week after he got back from R and R."

He had come to her office, past the lineup of soldiers waiting to file their forms at her desk, had studied every regulation hanging on the blow-torched plywood walls of her office as if he'd never seen them before. Then, finally, when they were alone: "Can I see you?"

And he had driven her in the S-Five Jeep like a man possessed, her hair whipping in the hot breeze as he roared past the airstrip and its repair shops and hangars and "fuel farm," past supply sheds, motor pools, tank parks, barracks and mess halls and sandbagged trench lines, out past the shantytown that GIs called Dogpatch where tens of thousands of refugees made do with what Americans threw away. At last he pulled to a stop beyond the barbed wire perimeter on an open patch of ferociously hot, barren red earth not conducive to VC ambush, but Kate had already strapped on a .45 for protection and carried Cap's rifle across her lap.

He turned off the engine, took the rifle from her, and then broke his silence. "Third MPs pulled a raid last night."

"I heard," she said. This was nothing new—every kind of drug was obtainable in Dogpatch and the MPs from Third Marines conducted random forays which produced absolutely no change in the drug supply.

"My quarters too," he said.

She was surprised. "Yours?"

"I think somebody spread some disinformation. Payback for putting the water buffalo shooting on report."

"Nobody got punished—"

"Everybody got official reprimands."

"Big deal. Anyway, you're not a drug user, you were clean, right?"

"Not exactly." Never taking his eyes from the surrounding terrain, he shook his head. "They found . . ."

He cleared his throat. She saw his confidence, his vitality, every ounce of his bravado, recede; he looked deflated, almost shrunken in his perspiration-soaked green fatigues.

"Pictures." His shoulders heaved with his sigh. "Pictures from Sydney."

He had spent his R & R in Australia. She was not quite sure she wanted him to elaborate, but she nodded encouragement.

He propped the rifle on the Jeep's door, fingering the catch. "I was stupid enough to bring back photos.

138 KATHERINE V. FORREST

And a fancy piece of underwear . . . somebody bought me."

She felt broiled in the sun, as if her blood were congealing in her veins. She asked carefully, "What exactly did he give you?"

He snapped a look at her that conveyed such gratitude for her use of the pronoun that she had to turn away.

"A pair of bikini shorts with a fairy godmother on the crotch."

She had to bite her cheeks to stifle a bark of laughter, then quickly sobered again. "The MPs—what did they say? What did you say?"

"I told them it was a joke gift for my sister. They just nodded. They were, like . . . the last place on earth those three guys wanted to be was in my quarters."

"Well, your explanation sounds . . . plausible," said Kate.

"It would be if I had a sister," he said, pulling his cap down over his eyes.

He was more bereft of family than she. She at least had a father. Cap had never seen his. His mother had taken her intellectually gifted young son with her to Indiana and then died there of breast cancer. He could claim only a few aunts, uncles, and cousins in Tennessee whom he had not seen since he was a child.

"If it was just the shorts, Kate . . . But the photos. The MPs picked them up and dropped them like they were grenades . . ."

"Because everybody admires you."

He waved that off. "You're the only person I can

trust. You won't shoot me in the back or toss a grenade in my bunk because I'm a faggot.''

She managed a smile. "I notice you took the rifle from me.''

"You don't have to tell me I'm stupid, Kate. I was going to toss the stuff, but I was only back a week, I thought I could keep it just a little while longer. . . .''

The loneliness in him was as deep as it was in her. She reached to him, took his hand.

Squeezing her hand almost painfully, he said, "I'm out on a limb anybody can saw off. I'm on the brass's shit list, Maloney hates my guts—''

"Everybody else likes you, admires you. Dacey says it took real balls to report the water buffalo shooting.''

"Everybody hates queers, he will too, when he hears . . .''

She doubted that very much; Dacey seemed almost infatuated with Cap. "Queers maybe,'' she conceded, "but not you,'' she said.

"You're deluding yourself,'' Cap said.

"Let's go get a drink.'' Kate took the rifle from Cap and placed it again across her lap. "And talk.''

That evening was the drunkest night of her life. The two of them had sat in the bone-chilling air-conditioning of the Officers' Club, blessed relief from the fierce sun and dusty air, then out on the veranda, talking late into the night, heads together, drinking without pause, and quietly exchanging life histories with raw and complete honesty. Two days later, Cap had bought the ring at the PX, and they had announced their engagement. The ring today lay in her special metal box along with her dog tags.

"He found out there was speculation over his sexual identity," Kate told Carver and Duffy. "We got engaged to help each other out, to keep people off our backs."

And because I loved him with a clear and deep and uncomplicated love that I've never felt for anyone, before or since. Because he loved me the same way. Because we loved each other.

"So, what happened?" Carver asked "How did he turn up missing?"

Not trusting her voice, she took time to pour a cup of coffee before she said, "He was rotated out of S-Five, a normal rotation. But to Khe Sanh, near the Demilitarized Zone. He'd put two officers on report when they shot a Vietnamese family's water buffalo for sport, and I suspect friends of theirs in the Officer Corps deliberately put him in harm's way to retaliate. But he was glad to get away to anywhere new. And I was glad he'd know somebody up there—since that's where Allan Gerlock was."

She took a sip of coffee. "Cap's second day there," she said, "two Marine Corps officers made official notification to me as his fiancée that he'd gone out on his first patrol and was missing in action." She had spoken just as calmly now as she had back then; she had not believed then that he was dead, she did not believe it now.

"After twenty-five years," Carver said thoughtfully, "from what you say, he figures to be dead, either by friend or by foe . . . which you're unwilling to concede. The only other alternatives are that he's a prisoner or a deserter."

She shrugged. "Okay, I'll tell you. The CAP program completely disillusioned him. He knew firsthand how much the South Vietnamese actually loathed their government. He knew better than anybody that we had no business over there. I don't know how he'd get out of Nam as a deserter, but with his beliefs it's what he needed to do, and he was smart and resourceful. If he did manage it, he'd never be able to contact me safely. He wouldn't take a chance on implicating his fiancée as an accomplice."

"This country gave amnesty to deserters," Carver reminded her in a quiet tone.

"Yes." And how she had hoped and wished that amnesty would bring him out of hiding. "Maybe by then he just wanted it all behind him. God knows I did."

Kate added musingly, "He told me something once. Said he was giving four years of his life in service to his country because he loved his country unconditionally. And after he fulfilled that commitment he figured that this dutiful son had demonstrated everything he ever needed to prove to anyone."

She looked at Duffy, then at Carver. "I don't know what happened to Cap, maybe realizing his love of country was no longer unconditional broke all of his ideals, maybe he thought his conditional love for his country had no value to anyone. Maybe I'll never know. But he gave me the reason to put in my own four years, and I did it."

Neither Carver nor Duffy spoke. She could feel something emanating from them, perhaps sympathy, or worse—pity.

She thought: *But afterward I never did lay full claim to*

my life, I still didn't think I'd earned it. I left the Marine Corps and went back into hiding . . . and maybe Cap did exactly the same.

She stirred restlessly. She wanted to get out of here. Right now she needed those people upstairs in her suite. They were eyewitnesses to a vital part of her life; she needed to be with them now, to hear their voices.

"By the way, Kate," Duffy said almost casually, "some information about David Olson, the desk clerk. Claims he observed everyone who went up or down in the elevator, everyone who left the hotel and came back, from the time Allan Gerlock checked in. What's your opinion—can we trust that information?"

"I'd say so. He's observant and conscientious. It figures he'd be more so after my room was shot into."

"Olson claims he didn't see anybody go up in the elevators who wasn't a guest of the hotel," Carver said. "Based on that, one of the people we've sent up to your room is our killer."

Kate sat perfectly still. Whoever had killed Allan Gerlock had killed one of the last men to see Cap Pearson alive. . . .

"None of them are fully alibied for either today or yesterday," Duffy said. "We think you're in danger. Until we develop an angle on this, maybe there's safety in numbers."

"Any ideas? Any suspects?" Kate asked, rubbing her eyes. What a misery of a night.

"Other than yourself?" Carver asked with his embalmed smile, and she did not imagine for a moment that he was joking, that she had been crossed completely off Carver's mental list. Nor should she be.

Even good cops cracked under pressure, and there were surely some bad cops. And there were other cops, like those she had observed at the criminal profiling seminar, who seemed separated from their own latent criminality by the thinnest of membranes.

Duffy said, "The shooting in your room, we're looking into that again, we've been down to look at that room. We think somebody was sending a message. They killed Gerlock, but you—you they sent a message to. Maybe they were smart enough not to blow away a cop, maybe they knew we'd come after a cop-killer with everything we have."

"My aunt Martha could have offed this guy," Carver said, "given the element of surprise. I like this Melanie Shaw, she's a . . ."

Bitch, Kate mentally filled in.

". . . she has the right degree of nastiness," Carver finished.

"I like Woody Hampton," Duffy said. "I don't think he's just styling in those military duds. Anybody running around in military drag twenty-five years after he doesn't have to—he's got John Wayne syndrome. Ex-Doctor Coleman is a good possible, he looks about seven eighths nut to me."

"Rachel Summers," said Carver. "Still waters run deep."

"You like the women, I like the men," Duffy told his partner. "So to speak," he added under his breath. "But then there's Gabriel Bradford—another still water in my book."

Kate felt bruised by these casually damning assessments of people who had loomed so large in her life.

Especially Rachel. She asked, "Are those five the only ones you have any vibes about?"

"If you can even call them vibes," Carver said, rubbing a hand over his chin. "Nothing quite that definite. Dacey never even met the victim. Doctor Goldberg—I can't imagine a motive. A solid gold citizen, he seems to have less in common with this group than anyone. Kate, we're just hoping to have a suspect, or a lead to a suspect, by the time you and Miss Grant return to Los Angeles."

Kate was half-listening. What Carver had said about Martin Goldberg was so true that she wondered why Martin had bothered to come here.

"What about Bernie?" she asked. "Bernadette O'Rourke Murphy."

"I hope not," Duffy said. "I like her. An Irish mother, as played by Robin Williams."

The men chuckled, and Kate smiled, knowing that Bernie herself would laugh at Duffy's remark.

"This case is sure different," Carver conceded. "A real mystery sneaks into town in between the usual domestic violence and drug snuff-outs."

"Travel plans . . ." Duffy consulted his notebook. "Everybody's committed to being in the city until tomorrow night. After that, Bernadette Murphy, Rachel Summer, Doctor Goldberg, and Gabriel Bradford will be leaving, the rest of you are here till Monday."

Kate offered cautiously, "If you're telling me that a man missing in action for twenty-five years is somehow involved in this whole thing, then I'll ask all the questions I can about Cap."

"I can't even guess how he could be involved," said

Carver, "but I can tell you that he somehow is."

She admired his professionalism and his determination to hold on to the reins of this case. He would not move an inch toward revealing to her the initials he had found under Allan Gerlock's hand. She walked to the bar and helped herself to two bottles of Cutty Sark and two of Smirnoff. "This may get some tongues loosened," she said.

"From what I hear, a lot of the Vietnam vets could never get their lives back together," Duffy said, dolefully eyeing the booze she carried. "I read somewhere that more than half of them have died violently—suicides or homicides. I wish the courts today would do what they did about Dacey back then—told him he could either go to jail or let the Marines try and straighten him out. He seems very together, a personable guy who's made something of himself."

Dacey? Kate made a mental note to ask him about his success.

"This particular group looks like normal America to me," Duffy concluded.

"Except for one," Carver said, opening the door of the Concord Room.

Kate nodded to the officer guarding the lobby as she glanced toward the front desk; David Olson was not there. She peered through the front door at the street and sighed. Rain was sweeping in windblown sheets across the pavement. Just like the monsoon months of her time in Vietnam.

12

HEARING Kate's card key engage the lock, Aimee hurried to the door of the suite before it opened, before displeasure could form in Kate's eyes at her presence in this room. Aimee said, "The phone rang, I picked it up. It was Torrie." She had answered, of course, because she knew Kate had left for another interview with the detectives.

Kate glanced at her watch. "It's eight o'clock back there. What's up?"

"Lieutenant Bodwin called her, filled her in on what's going on. She wishes to heaven she could be here with you. I told her I wished the same thing." Aimee was certain that Kate wished she could be anywhere but here, trapped in an investigation of a murder over which she had no control or jurisdiction.

"Did she mention the case she's working?"

"What's going on here is all we talked about." She thought remorsefully: *And I know more about that than I have any right to know.*

"So you're telling me I don't have to call her tonight," Kate said, stepping aside as Bernie emerged from the bathroom, and Melanie, next in the procession, took her place.

Aimee was used to Kate's meticulous approach to anything connected with her work. "Torrie said she'd talk to you tomorrow if you have time. Let me take those," she said, reaching for the bottles in Kate's arms. She would assist Kate with the role of hostess and then disappear. In just the last few minutes the rain had increased; no way would she overhear from the bedroom what was going on—nor did she want to hear.

To Aimee's exasperation, Kate was gazing doubtfully at the telephone. As if she didn't have enough to contend with, now she was wondering whether she should call her partner back.

"Honey," Bernie said to Aimee, "I'll get extra glasses from our room, why don't you tell that nice officer in the hallway you need to fill up the ice bucket."

"Sure," Aimee said.

When she returned with the ice, Bernie had deposited four glasses and was rushing out again. Kate was seated at the table by the window. Martin Goldberg, having surrendered Kate's place back to her, evidently preferred to lean against the wall beside Gabe rather than sit next to Doc on the sofa. Smoking a long, thin cigarette in a small silver holder, a model of flawless attire in cream-colored gabardine slacks and a powder-blue pullover that accented his tanned face, the doctor was smiling at Kate. "So they didn't handcuff and torture you."

Kate's half-smile was an acknowledgment of Aimee's return, not of Martin or his comment. "They didn't handcuff me," she answered him.

Bernie came bustling back, a young uniformed officer in her wake, both of them carrying chairs, evidently from Bernie's room. The cop deposited his
burden and after a quick, amused grin at Bernie, left
the suite.

As Aimee edged toward the door to the bedroom,
Bernie said, "Where are you off to?"

"I'm a little tired," she said. She remembered when
she was a child, begging to be allowed to sit with
grown-ups, desperate to understand the superiority
and mystery of them. The shared experience of the
generation in this room was completely beyond her,
had nothing to do with her; she was clearly an interloper who did not belong here.

"Don't be silly, you're too young to be tired," Bernie
said. "Sit down, have a drink."

"Yes, join us," Rachel insisted.

"I'd be glad to see you stay," Dacey said sincerely.

About to again demur, Aimee looked at Kate for support. But found instead a plea on her face: *Please—I
need you here.* Nodding to Kate, she resignedly perched
on the arm of the sofa away from the group, near the
door to the bedroom.

She watched the room take on a new configuration:
Martin inserting one of the chairs between Bernie and
Melanie at the table; Dacey grabbing the other and
swinging it over beside the window, where he sat
astride it, back to front, folding his arms along its top.

In typical cop fashion, Kate now sat at the end of
the room on the far side of the table, her back to the
wall, facing into the room so that she could observe
everyone. At the table on each side of her were Bernie

and Woody, with Martin and Melanie across from her, all of them except Kate drinking bourbon or scotch. Dacey, accepting the drink handed to him by Woody, sat adjacent to Kate in front of the window; Rachel reclined on the floor beside the sofa, her back against the side wall. Doc sprawled on the sofa; Gabe continued to stand, his cap pushed back on his head, his legs apart, hips braced against the wall, a drink in one hand, cigarette in the other.

Martin said, "God knows how long the cops will keep us here. Five different sets of police in this town, it's still the worst city on earth. You hear all these horror stories about the police station downtown—"

"They've got five different police forces?" Melanie asked incredulously. "Why?"

"Different jurisdictions. The Park Police—they have all the federal grounds. The Capitol Police—"

"Spiffy-looking," Aimee commented, remembering the crisp white shirts and shiny brass fittings of the uniformed police who had seemed polite and mostly inconspicuous amid the overwhelming display of statuary, marble, mosaic-style tile, intricate bronze trim, heroic-size portraits, vast ceilings, pillars and columns of the United States Capitol.

"Monitors for the tourists," Martin scoffed, waving his cigarette. "Then there's EPS, the Executive Protective Service, they keep the riffraff away from Embassy Row. The Monuments, they're patrolled by the uniformed division of the Secret Service. Let me tell you, if any one of those outfits ever had to investigate a real crime, they'd have to call in a real cop. The D.C. police try their best, they're buried in . . ." Martin searched for a word.

"Horseshit? Corruption?" Doc supplied. "Politics?"

"All one and the same," Woody commented, pouring the Cutty Sark freely into his glass and Martin's. He had pressed another saucer into use as an ashtray.

Martin nodded. "Cynicism is the truth of this town. Washington used to be a magnificent city—now it's drug wars and murder and mayhem, it's thieving bureaucrats and real estate fraud, it's Congress tut-tutting over corruption and getting in limos and driving home to Virginia. The crime rate—Kate, you must know this—it's there with the highest in the country—"

"It is."

"Infant mortality is something you'd expect in the third world. The school system—we spend more money than any other city and it's still putrid—"

"Drink your scotch, Martin," Bernie said. "Watch your blood pressure."

"The scumbags running this town couldn't manage a Burger King. Everything's a disaster, nothing works, everything's falling apart, the police are overwhelmed and demoralized like every other civil servant—"

"I must tell you," Kate said, "the officers I've dealt with seem very competent and professional. I suspect they're like most cops everywhere—they do their best whatever the circumstances."

"Youth is to discover," Bernie murmured, "age is to compare . . ."

"Who are you quoting?" Doc asked with interest. He had taken off his baseball cap and sat with legs crossed, an arm along the back of the sofa, smoke curling up from the cigarette between his fingers. Both of these medical doctors, Aimee observed, were heavy smokers.

Bernie turned in her chair to peer back at Doc. "Beats me. I use it to remind myself. When I was a kid every older person I knew claimed the world was going straight to hell in a handbasket. Things aren't worse, they're just different. We've turned into the same kind of tiresome, boring old poops our grandparents were."

Stifling the impulse to shout agreement, Aimee smiled privately and remembered her first day in this city. Going by herself to stand in coldly brilliant sunshine in Lafayette Park, its park benches and carefully tended flower beds lining immaculate patches of lawn, gazing for a long time across Pennsylvania Avenue, past the array of homeless trudging back and forth, past the wrought-iron fencing to the emerald lawn and the glowing whiteness of a structure that looked smaller than the White House of her imagination, but which nonetheless thrilled her to the marrow.

"There's no city anywhere as bad as Washington, D.C.," Martin said.

"Do you live in the city?" Melanie said.

He looked at her. "Of course not."

Rachel said with clear irony, "We're not in Da Nang anymore, Martin."

"Damn right," said Woody, looking at Rachel for an additional clue as to her meaning.

"But anyone would think we were. A friend of ours died here tonight."

Martin's face remained impassive; his thick gray mustache twitched. "Look, I haven't seen the man in twenty-five years. His death has nothing to do with me. Thank God."

Exhaling two thin streams of smoke through his nostrils, he waved off the subject of Allan Gerlock and of Washington, D.C. "What are these cops telling you, Kate?"

"Not much," she said. "They wanted to know about Cap and me."

I'd sure like to know about that too, Aimee thought.

Martin asked, "Why?"

"I don't know, Martin."

Kate's answer sounded to Aimee like the truth rather than one of her smooth deflections.

"For God's sake, Katie," Bernie said, "you're a cop, why aren't they including you in on things?"

"It doesn't count here."

Gabe said, "I think they're looking anyplace for a motive for this. Why anybody would go after Allan—"

"Or Kate," Rachel said. "Kate was shot at—"

"It all has to be connected," Martin said sharply. "Maybe Allan somehow got in the way of somebody coming after Kate."

"That doesn't make any sense—"

"Well, what that has to do with Cap—"

Woody raised his voice over all others to say to Kate, "I think they're trying to figure out about you showing up here with a girlfriend. Funny, Allan always claimed Rachel was the lesbo. But you—"

"Woody," Rachel said amid general exclamations of dismay and disgust, "you're such a . . . stereotype."

As the room erupted in laughter, Woody grinned uncertainly. "Hey, I wasn't slamming anybody, I got no problems about you or Kate, I think you're all great. Aimee too.''

"Peachy," Rachel said.

"So," Dacey said, "what about Cap?"

"What about him," Kate returned, rubbing her eyes tiredly.

"Have a drink, Katie," Bernie said, "you need one."

"Is there any more coffee?"

"I'll call downstairs," Aimee said.

When she hung up from her request to the wearily cooperative desk clerk, Woody, teetering on the back legs of his chair, was regaling the group.

"Here we were, coming back from the NCO club, drunk as skunks, and Dacey smacks the fuckin' Jeep into a nurses' hooch. Lieutenant Jarvis is the first one outta there—"

"Tearing out with just her pajama bottoms on," Dacey chortled, banging a hand on his chair back, "boobs bouncing like grapefruits—"

"Screamin' her head off, a flak jacket over her head—"

"Chicken Little with the sky falling—"

"I didn't care if they threw us in the brig, it was worth it," howled Woody, wiping his eyes.

"So it was you guys," Rachel said, laughing along with everyone else. "Poor Lorraine, any noise at all she thought a shell was landing on her—"

"Hell, I did too," Bernie said.

"Yes, but you didn't sleep under your bed—"

"*I* did," Kate said.

"Well, you didn't line your room with sandbags—"

"Never thought of it or I would have," Kate said, to more laughter.

"I don't think Lorraine slept a night through the whole time she was over there."

Aimee was staring at Kate. So Vietnam had been a year in limbo, had it? A year at the rear of the war, away from infantry assaults and air strikes, the only enemies rain and heat and boring routine?

But Kate was focused on Woody as he went on, "Well, that Lorraine gal was a brick. She hadn't covered for us, we'd of been in the brig for sure."

"Or maybe the highest ranking Marines that ever burned shitters," Dacey said, slapping the chair again.

"What's he talking about?" Aimee asked Doc sotto voce, amid the hilarity.

Grinning, Doc shook his head. "The worst punishment on a military base, Aimee. The poor devils had to collect these big drums of feces from the outhouses, take them to special burning points and set them on fire."

"When the wind was blowing the wrong way—phew," Rachel contributed.

"No appreciating the aroma of shitters burning," said Melanie, "unless you were there."

"No appreciating anything about Nam unless you were there," Gabe said.

"Some things even if you were there, you had to do 'em," Woody said meaningfully, and flicked ash from his cigarette into a saucer-ashtray with a snap of his thumbnail.

"Woody, goddammit, cut the crap," snapped Melanie. "I'm sick of you guys acting like women didn't come close to what you guys went through over there. Like we didn't have our asses on the line every bit as much as you did—"

"Hear, hear," said Rachel.

"Well, you didn't, that's the—"

"Listen," Melanie commanded. "Just listen, okay? I was all over the fucking place. I was in combat as much as any of you guys except they wouldn't let me have a gun so I could shoot back. I was in Cu Chi and Chu Lai, and it was hell. I got shot at I don't know how many times in helicopters. I was in the line of fire"— she jabbed a finger toward Bernie and then Rachel— "a lot more than Saint Bernadette and Mother Teresa over here—"

Kate said, "Come off it, Melanie—"

"Stay the fucking hell out of this, Kate. You never put your ass on the line, not much wonder you had to be tricked into coming here, all you did over there was sit in your goddamn office—"

"*Hey!*" Aimee's shock finally coalesced into fury.

"Fucking *horseshit*, Melanie," Bernie snarled, waving at Aimee as if to say she would handle this. "We got mortared and shelled every goddamn night—"

"We were all in it," Rachel said calmly. "VC shells didn't know any difference between Kate and the rest of us. Neither did the fever that landed Kate in the hospital—"

Fever? Again Aimee stared at Kate, but remained silent, knowing she must not interfere.

"All of us were fucking sitting ducks." Bernie spoke less harshly, Rachel's tone seeming to have affected her.

Kate offered nothing further to a sudden and awkward silence; instead, looking tense and edgy, she cast glances at every occupant of the room except Aimee, and at the fresh drink sitting in front of Bernie. Bernie's untouched bourbon reminded Aimee uncomfortably of Kate's drinking pattern: tossing scotch down quickly, then pouring a drink which she sipped intermittently, as if to hold on to the effect she had attained. These days, getting to that sip-from drink was requiring a larger and larger initial quantity of scotch. Kate choosing not to drink in order to remain alert would accomplish nothing if that in itself became a distraction.

"Shells coming in, remember, Rach?" Bernie finally said. "Here we are in the ward and we're supposed to put on helmets and flak jackets, and I'd like to know how you could take care of patients wearing a goddamn flak jacket—"

"Or how you could run to a bunker because shells were landing," Rachel said. "How you could leave patients—"

Doc said, "I remember coming into the ward after a generator blew and here's Bernie and Rachel moving those guys to other beds, just picking them up and moving them—"

"Bernie did most of that," Rachel said.

"I was always a strong broad," Bernie said, grinning as she flexed a solid-looking muscle in her arm.

A knock on the door. Aimee opened it to the desk clerk, who glanced into the room and took one staggering step backward, his mouth an O of dismay. "This is a nonsmoking—"

"Yes, we know, I'm sorry."

"Oh, Moses . . ." Rolling his eyes upward, he passed the tray of coffee to Aimee.

"Thank you, David," Kate called.

Mumbling indecipherably, he backed out the door, staring until it closed on him.

Bernie was saying to Rachel, "Remember Joanie and Karen, the frag wounds they got on the way to the MARS station?"

"MARS was the Military Affiliate Radio Station," Gabe whispered to Aimee.

"Thanks," Aimee whispered back.

Kate overheard the exchange between Gabe and Aimee with approval. The normally taciturn Gabe speaking up was proof that Aimee's outsider presence was valuable; she could help by drawing out the people in this room, and some clue to Allan Gerlock's death could well emerge.

"Phones," Dacey further clarified to Aimee in a normal tone, smiling. "You could call back to the World, just like E.T." His smile faded. "If you had anybody to call."

Kate had gone to the MARS station only once. Bouncing over a pitch-black road in a Jeep, in the dead calm of a hot, humid night because of the time difference between Nam and the States, accompanying three utterly silent Marines with M-16s at the ready, listening for any alien sound in the darkness.

Then placing the phone call to her father, engendering stark panic in him: "Kate, what's wrong—" "Nothing, Dad—" "What's *wrong?*" "I swear to you nothing's wrong—" But there was indeed something wrong—her father's voice had unleashed an assault of homesickness so debilitating that she could barely navigate her way through the phone call, so distinct was her image of him in the family room where her parents had spent most evenings of her life, her mother sewing, her father reading his gardening magazines or watching television. Her father would be taking this phone call in his dark brown recliner, shoulder holding the receiver to his ear, fingers absently stroking the frayed plaid arm covers that Kate's mother had made for his chair one scant month before her death. Afterward, Kate had not called again, even at Christmas, had settled for sending letters and an occasional audiotape.

"Joanie and Karen were damn lucky," Bernie said. "A piece of shrapnel just missed Karen's jugular, remember? They were back at work in a couple of days and got themselves a couple of Purple Hearts out of it."

Rachel said, "I remember the sapper attacks, those poor boys—"

"Christ on the cross, they were VC," hissed Dacey, gripping the back of his chair and glaring down at Rachel where she sat on the floor. "Out to blow our ammo dumps and all of us sky-high."

"Dacey, get a little perspective. They were children, every one of them shot to pieces before they even got through the barbed wire."

"They were fuckin' gooks with explosives strapped to their bodies," Woody said.

"They were human beings," Doc said, and Kate could hear the tremor in his voice.

"They were gooks," Dacey said.

"So it's still that easy to kill. Nonwhite lives are still as cheap as chaff," Rachel said softly.

Melanie said, "It happens every day, Mary Poppins. You only *think* you've left Da Nang."

"It's what happened here tonight to Allan," Gabe said.

Woody said, "You doctors, with your hypocritic oath—"

"Hippocratic," Martin said with a wan smile.

"Whatever damn thing it is, I guess I can understand an oath—"

"We had to take care of them," Rachel said to Dacey. "For the reason Doc gave."

"Back then we were doctors and nurses pure and simple," Bernie said. She picked up her bourbon. "Healing was what we did."

"Within regulations, of course," Doc said bitterly. "Let's not forget our orders. Top priority was American soldiers, second priority was American dogs, then came the North Vietnam Army soldiers and the Vietcong. After that, South Vietnamese troops and civilians."

"Dogs?" Aimee blurted. "Dogs and enemy soldiers came before allies and civilians?"

"Dogs were trained, and expensive. Enemy troops could have useful information. So, you see, we did things far worse than taking care of Vietcong," Doc said.

"What the hell are you talking about?" Dacey demanded. "Our *orders* were to *kill* them. Yours should have been the same goddamn thing."

"Drop it, I don't want to hear any more about this," Martin said, shaking his head as if the motion could obliterate his sense of hearing.

"Wimps. Pollyannas, all of you," Melanie said with a dismissive wave toward the medical profession end of the room. "If you'd been out there on the lines with the guys like I was—"

"You're right, Melanie," Rachel said, "all we saw were the atrocious casualties afterward."

"Listen, Mother Teresa," Melanie said, jabbing a finger on the table as she glared down at her, "you weren't with those boys, you didn't see their eyes, their faces when they got orders to take a hill, go into a village. Our men fought the enemy, you gave aid and comfort—"

"Melanie, Melanie—" Bernie stuttered in her fury.

Kate struggled to remain silent. She wanted to pour Melanie's drink over her head.

Rachel said, "Did you ever have one of your heroes show you body pieces he'd cut off Vietcong corpses?"

"Are you kidding?" Melanie retorted. "They showed me everything. They could've carried fucking VC heads around on posts for all I cared."

"They almost did," Rachel said. "One time a guy showed me a scalp." She got up from the floor. "I need a drink."

Kate was remembering again the first time she had seen Dacey, when he had climbed off the helicopter in the triage area, and what he had worn around his neck that had looked like dried leaves, and later learning from a disgusted Bernie what they were.

"They showed me everything too," Bernie said. "Fingers, toes—"

"Ears," Kate said, looking at Dacey. "They wore necklaces made of VC ears."

"Barbaric," Bernie said.

Dacey looked back at Kate, blank-eyed.

"Heroic," said Melanie.

"A sniper we shot out of a tree," Woody said flatly, "the fucker blew two of us away, we cut the fucker's balls off."

"No soldier ever showed me anything like a body part," Doc said, looking to Martin for his reaction. But Martin had removed the cigarette from his holder and was focused on stubbing it out. "Gabe," Doc said, "you didn't do things like that."

"The VC mutilated people in the villages all the time," Gabe said. "Chopped arms off little kids, cut breasts off women—"

"But *you* didn't do things like that."

"It was a . . . rite," Gabe said, crossing his arms tightly over his chest. "You had to take something. Everybody did."

"Jesus," Doc said.

"Dream on, Pollyanna," Melanie muttered.

"All my father brought home from the war was a German pistol," Bernie said to Kate.

"Mine too," said Kate.

"Don't be too sure they didn't collect some other stuff," said Dacey. "War is war, you do what you do."

Her father? Cut off someone's ears or penis?

"With all due respect to you women," Gabe added, "war's always been men's work—"

"So is murder," Aimee blurted.

"And assault and rape and every other foul thing on earth," Bernie added.

"Horseshit," declared Woody. He jabbed a finger at Bernie, then at Kate, at Rachel, at Melanie. "You, you, you, you—" After an instant's hesitation he included Aimee in his finger-jabbing, "—and you. All of you could have killed Allan. Any one of you women could carve somebody's nuts off just as easy as any of us."

Gabe continued doggedly, "With all due respect, ninety-nine point nine percent of those names on the Wall are ours—your own Phyllis Schlafly's said that women have done useful things, but we've won wars because we had brave men who killed the enemy—"

"With all due respect to you, Gabe, and none to Mrs. Schlafly or to Woody," Rachel said, pouring scotch into a glass, "there were worse things in Vietnam than dying."

"Oh, come *off* it," Melanie jeered.

"Like what?" Dacey demanded. "Name one."

Rachel stood in front of Dacey's chair, drink in hand, gazing at him. "Did you ever imagine what it was like having to look into all those black bags your friend Will Maloney hauled back on his dustoff? We had to, every single one of them, because somebody needed to write something down about what was in those bags, something to tell the families . . ."

Rachel turned away from Dacey and made her way to the sofa and sat between Doc and Aimee as Bernie said, "Same thing in the wards. We had to prepare each soldier for Graves Registration. I don't know how many dead young boys we had to zip into body bags . . .'' She trailed off.

"One time," Gabe said softly, shifting his hips against the wall and gazing down at the bright end of his cigarette, "one time we went in after a real bad firefight. Of all the damn things for the Marine Corps to screw up, we ran out of body bags. Had to stack guys in the helicopter, pile them up like cordwood—"

"Will brought some in like that," Dacey said. "Puked his guts out all over his chopper. Had to go back twice for more bodies."

"We're not saying you gutsy women did anything but a great job," Woody said. "But it's nothing like a firefight. The noise, the fucking terror—"

Bernie's head snapped up. "You ever been in an operating room with incoming wounded, Woody? Let me tell you about noise and fucking terror. The wounded packed in so tight there's hardly any space, you can't walk anywhere that you don't leave bloody footprints, the floors so slick after a while you can hardly walk at all, and after you finally sort through the dead and get the wounded taken care of, your scrubs are soaked right through to your skin and you can't even hope to clean those floors any other way but to use a garden hose to sluice out all the gore."

Kate wondered if Aimee was as sick as she looked.

"Ah, bad, yeah, that's real bad," Woody said, shaking his head. He looked at Bernie with eyes so vulnerable that to Kate he suddenly no longer looked like a middle-aged man wearing military fatigues but a boy dressed up in a costume. "How about watching your closest buddy get it right in front of your eyes like Gary did. Seeing him trigger a Bouncing Betty—"

"Gary?" Rachel said, a slender hand at her throat. "What was his last name?"

"Hamlin."

"Did he die?" Martin asked gently.

"Yeah. After a while. You guys couldn't save him." Woody pushed his chair away from the table and walked quickly through the room and into the bathroom.

Rachel took several audible gulps of her drink. Martin said, "Bad as Woody feels, his friend is better off." He addressed Aimee: "A Bouncing Betty is a mine that bounces waist-high, blows mortar fragments and anything else around it—dirt, sticks, stones—right through your skin. Any poor devil who lived through a Bouncing Betty, he'd be in for lifelong disabilities and complications."

"Martin, you don't know about Gary," Bernie said, staring into the depths of her drink. "A medic got to Gary before he could bleed to death and bagged him . . ."

"What is this?" Dacey said. "I don't know about this."

"Nobody does," Bernie said. "Except me and Rachel."

Inspecting what was left of her own drink, Rachel said, "Gary was a train wreck. It took a miracle that he'd lived this long. Unconscious, almost nothing left of his lower extremities, no way to take that bag off without massive hemorrhage, no way he could survive. So I put him behind the screen with the other expectants, thinking, well, you know, he had only minutes

. . . So after we finish with the immediates, I go back there and he's still with us and conscious. I can tell by his eyes he's figured out the shape he's in. So I slide my arms under his shoulders and he tells me his name and asks me to stay with him, and then I just hold him, and he says the Our Father, and I tell him everything's going to be better, and I'm unfastening the bag, and I'm holding him . . .''

This is too hard, Aimee thought, staring through a film of tears down into her lap. Too hard for me and way too hard for Rachel and Kate and everybody else in here.

She knew that Kate had arranged for these people to be gathered together here. She knew somebody could say something that would lead to a reason why Allan Gerlock had been murdered tonight, and what lay behind the shots fired into their own room. But God, this was just too hard.

Wiping tears from her cheeks she looked up. Bernie was refilling Rachel's glass, and Kate—Kate was fixated on Rachel and on Doc. Doc, who sat still as death on the sofa beside her.

Woody came out of the bathroom still adjusting his belt. Rachel would not look at him. Aimee stared at him, at his red-rimmed eyes. Surely Rachel—or some-one—would now tell him his best friend had died com-forted in Rachel's arms.

Gabe cleared his throat and said, ''It was real tough on you women, I know that. But we—''

''With all due respect,'' Melanie said, repeating with clear irony the phrase Gabe and Rachel had used earlier to each other. "Let me tell you something, Gabe. And you too, Dacey. And Woody. We know how tough it was for you guys, how brutal. All the women in this room, even Aimee, we know your stories from how many newspapers? How many movies? How many books?" She gestured to Rachel and Bernie, to herself. "Nobody knows our stories. One fucking TV series about what we did—"

"Listen," Dacey said. "The truth is, we did fight to protect you women, you were back out of danger—"

"Fuck that for a joke," Melanie retorted.

Bernie said, "One night I'm walking through one of the units that's right off the helicopter pad, a mortar comes in, shrapnel whistling right past me, I mean screaming so close to my head my eardrums vibrate, it goes thudding into God knows what, I'm too busy trying to throw my ass into a bunker."

"Lorraine," Rachel said. "Lorraine's in a ward, at the medicine cabinet near the door, shrapnel blows right through the door, right through the tibia of a corpsman standing beside her."

"God, poor Lorraine, not much wonder she was scared to death," Melanie said with a half-grin. "I really tried not to be scared, no matter what. It always seemed the guys I knew who were the most petrified, they're the ones that bought it."

"Heat-seeking missiles, fear-seeking missiles," Martin murmured, holding his glass sideways and pouring whiskey cautiously, as if he expected it to foam up like beer.

"What I saw over there," Woody said to him, "the doctors could of been mechanics working on cars—fix 'em up, send 'em right back out on the road."

Martin did not reply.

"The real men over there carried guns, not knives," Woody pushed on.

"Woody, cut it out," Gabe said softly.

Bernie said, "It was a butcher shop anywhere you were."

Rachel, who had still not looked at Woody, suddenly started to laugh, peals of shrieking laughter with an edge of hysteria. "I all of a sudden remembered Felicia," she gasped to Bernie.

"Felicia," Bernie said. "Oh, God, yes," and she went off into her own whoops of laughter.

"What, what?" said Dacey, grinning.

"Christ, it wasn't funny but it was," Bernie said, pawing at her eyes.

"Felicia's this brand-new nurse, okay? Just in-country, just off a C-130 from Tan Son Nhut, she comes in right after we get incoming wounded, bad stuff, a claymore mine, so there's amputations. And here's sweet young Felicia, all enthusiastic to check out her new hospital and meet her new team. So in she bounces, into our operating room, and we're finishing up and there's blood just fucking everywhere, and Martin's tying off this guy—he got choppered in with his arm all but hanging by a thread—and the deal is, I'm helping Martin and rummaging around for a bag—you put amputated limbs in special plastic bags, they go to Graves Registration for disposal just like bodies do. So anyway, here I am just busy as hell, but I notice Felicia, she's the color of putty from the scene in there but she's being a brave girl, she's gonna meet everybody no matter what. Then somebody says, 'This is Bernie O'Rourke,' and I turn around and my scrubs are dripping blood, and Felicia reaches out and shakes the one hand in the room that doesn't have a gory glove on it—and the hand's on this guy's arm that I fucking forget I'm holding, I've got it tucked under my arm, it's got tattoos all over it, and the poor bastard's wristwatch is still on it, and poor Felicia faints dead away on the floor.''

Aimee was holding her sides laughing; Martin was doubled over, so was Kate. Everyone was roaring with laughter.

"You guys are truly sick," Melanie said, wiping her eyes.

"Believe me, any one of us could have been Felicia," Rachel said, blotting her tears of laughter with a shirt sleeve.

"We were lots of us just like her, we went over there with all these starry-eyed Alice in Wonderland notions of helping our guys," Bernie said.

"For sure," Rachel said. "Just completely unprepared for anything like the carnage. Lots of us young, lots of us with no more than two years' experience—"

"The guys too—we didn't have any experience at all," Gabe pointed out.

Kate spoke. "The men were given training, Gabe—a mind-set for war. That applied even to me."

"The GMOs—" Martin spoke up.

"General Medical Officers," Doc supplied to Aimee.

"Most of us were interns—"

"Like me," Doc said.

"—or residents with very little experience, like I was.

I was made a captain with only a year of straight medical internship, one year of residency. Two years out of med school and handling all these horrendous casualties. Our GIs deserved better.''

"They did," Doc said. "They did."

"Triage was the worst," Rachel said, and she finally looked at Woody. "Every doctor in Nam had all they could do in the operating rooms, but imagine nurses barely out of their teens, hardly any experience, having to look at some boy barely out of *his* teens and deciding he was an expectant, having to put him behind a screen because he was going to die. And, Woody, I'm sorry about Gary, I had no idea he was your friend, I'm sorry I couldn't do anything for him—"

He looked at her, slack-jawed.

She said in a thick voice, "I didn't have any time to give anyone likely to die, I always had to take care of the immediates. At least I could be with him, holding him when he died . . .''

Ashen-faced, Woody said, "I heard somebody was with him, I didn't . . ." His fingers plucked at the Marine Corps insignia on the shirt of his fatigues. "Christ. I'm just glad it was you."

Rachel looked at Martin and said in a distant tone, "You're right, Martin, our GIs deserved better. They were boys, they were *kids*, and they died and we hardly even knew their *names* . . ." She whispered, "It was obscene.''

Aimee sat with her head bowed. Briefly, Doc patted her knee.

"*China Beach*," Bernie said. "That show at least got some of it right.''

"It didn't get the real China Beach right. We went there together, Kate, remember?" Rachel said.

"I do," Kate said, and Aimee looked up at her. "I couldn't watch the series. I found two hypo syringes sticking up in the sand, remember?"

"Sure. Not to mention bloody bandages and assorted garbage washing ashore from *Repose* and *Sanctuary*," Rachel finished, and half-smiled at her.

"Those were hospital ships in the South China Sea," Doc said to Aimee.

Dabbing at tears with a tissue, Aimee nodded.

Martin said, "Remember Rory Flynn?"

Rachel said, "Do I ever."

"Hey, I was the one who found him," Bernie said. "Came running to get him, he's sitting in a chair in his office, I'm yelling 'I've got a patient convulsing!' and he just sits there looking at me. And I'm yelling and yelling and yelling, I get right down into his face and I'm yelling—"

"He was such a terrific doctor," said Rachel. "Alan Alda in the flesh."

"He was," Martin said. "But he had a real bad run, one of those things that can happen to any of us, even here, even in private practice. I don't know how many men died on him, none of them his fault."

"What happened to the one with convulsions?" Kate asked Bernie.

"Died," she said.

"The doctor, what happened to him?" Aimee asked.

Martin said, "He was helicoptered out to one of the hospital ships and sent home."

"Rory Flynn just sat there looking at me," Bernie said.

"Doc," Kate said, "is this the reason you quit?"

"Remember Horatio?" Doc asked, turning to Bernie.

Rachel uttered a sound.

"Sure," Bernie said, gulping bourbon, "sure I do. The little kid Rachel and I specialed."

"Specialed?" Aimee ventured in a whisper to Doc.

Doc patted her knee again, a gesture that seemed both paternal and absentminded. "A little nine-year-old Vietnamese boy. His father brought him and just left him, walked away. The little fellow was a goner. Napalm—necrotic tissue over his entire head and chest. He managed to survive vasomotor collapse from shock, and that's when Bernie and Rachel took him over. Worked their full twelve-hour shift and then gave him their own time. The sensory nerve pain that little fellow suffered, then hypostatic pneumonia—"

"Imagine getting a sunburn on the inside of your lungs." Rachel seemed to be directing her soft-voiced explanation to Aimee, but Aimee wasn't sure; Rachel's eyes were following her own hand as it traced the crease in her pants. "Your lungs peel just like your skin."

Bernie said, "We did give up on him, Doc. We did. We just tried to give him some comfort. That little guy," she said, shaking her head in wonderment, "he'd cough from his toenails, a blood gusher out of his mouth—and so many times I'd hold him thinking this was it, he'd choke to death like so many of the napalms did."

Rachel said, "We called him Horatio because he was such a little battler. We'd given up, but he didn't. And then we wouldn't either. We were so proud of ourselves, we helped pull him through, we knew he'd have a lot of scar tissue, but—" Rachel broke off.

"We got word out to his family, they came to get him, all of them, maybe a dozen people," Doc said. "Fell all over themselves, they were so happy he was okay, and then the little kid tries to run to them and trips and falls and they see he's blind. We tell them we've fixed everything including starting skin grafts for his scars but there isn't anything we can do to give him back his sight, and they turn their backs on him and walk out."

"Barbarians," Melanie hissed. "Animals. You see? What did I tell you?"

"Peasants," Rachel said, sounding as if her throat were filled with tears. "Farmers with no way on God's earth of taking care of a blind child."

Aimee asked, unsure of whether she wanted to hear the answer, "So what happened to him?"

"The orphanage," said Bernie. "Run by three Vietnamese nuns so dedicated they should be canonized—"

"We went there with Cap," Rachel said. "Remember, Kate?"

"Of course," she said softly. She sat with elbows on the table, chin in hand, watching Doc.

Bernie said, "It was a ghastly warehouse for unwanted children. God only knows what happened after that. Best case, he's on the streets begging."

"Doc," Kate said, sitting up straight, "is this the reason?"

Doc looked at Martin as he said, "We were no more morally right in saving that boy's life than his Vietnamese family was morally wrong to abandon him."

"I'm only a doctor, not a philosopher," Martin said, inserting another cigarette into his silver holder. "But even I know that's completely simplistic."

Poor Doc, Aimee thought. If his conscience were any heavier, his head would roll off his shoulders.

"Your Horatio," Melanie said to Doc, "was probably a VC. One of those sweet little kids who'd dash past you and toss a grenade at your feet."

"Napalm burns were . . ." said Doc, as if he had not heard her. "They were . . ."

"I worked a burn ward for five weeks," Rachel said. "Janet, the head nurse, got me out of there before I went the way of Rory Flynn. The pain—you had to plead with patients to let you change dressings. The third degrees, I couldn't stand it." She shook her head. Eyes closed, she continued, "Some of them were so awful, so hopeless, they were crispy critters when they came in, but they hung on for days . . ."

Kate was enveloped by a cloud of smoke from Martin's cigarette; her nostrils felt coated by all the fumes in the room. "I thought that term was invented by ghoulish cops," she said. "Now I see it came out of Vietnam, if not earlier wars." She turned to Rachel. "You never told me about any of this."

"I never told anybody about a lot of things," Rachel replied.

"Remember how in Nam we never talked about anything to do with the war?" Bernie said, dumping two saucers full of ashes and butts into the wastebasket beside the table.

"Who could?" Rachel said. "You just existed, tried to get through it. Talking about it was the last thing in the world I ever wanted to do."

"Coming home made things worse," Bernie said. "Years, it was, like, ten years before I stopped keeping it secret that I'd been over there."

"I never thought about anybody but the government getting all the protests," Aimee murmured to Doc.

"My family didn't have a clue how damaged I was," Rachel said. "I was just paralyzed with grief, I desperately needed to talk. But my mother said everybody knew war was horrible." She paused. "She didn't want to hear about it."

"Good God," Aimee lamented.

"She knows now she was wrong." Rachel put a hand briefly on Aimee's knee as if she were the one who needed comforting. "Today we talk whenever I need to."

Bernie said bitterly, "Afterward, people I considered good friends cut me down because I served. I never forgave them, ever."

Woody said, "I thought I'd get some respect risking my life in that fucking place. So I come home and some fucking hippie at the airport asks how many people I killed, how it felt to kill people. I told him he was the one I'd enjoy killing."

"My father was in a complete rage," Kate said. "The TV news—he'd almost have apoplexy. He thought all the dissenters were traitors."

"I still do," Woody said. "Speaking of that draft-dodging asshole in the White House—"

"Woody, keep a lid on that stuff, okay?" Martin said.

"I'm with Woody," Dacey said.

"Me too," Melanie said.

"When I came home," Gabe said, "it was like time stopped while I was gone—everything was the same. But I wasn't."

Kate focused her gaze on the table in an attempt to regain some emotional equilibrium. Impossible that Carver and Duffy, or anyone, should expect her to sort out a motive for murder from the past being laid bare in this room. If there was a killer in the group, she had seen no clue as to who it might be.

"Everybody over there was so young," Kate said, still staring at the table so that her glance would not single out any individual. "Except for their eyes . . ."

"God yes," Rachel said, "the soldiers looked at us from such an incredible distance—"

So did the nurses and doctors, Kate thought.

"Yeah, the thousand-yard stare," Gabe said.

"Much further than that, Gabe," Martin said. "An uncrossable distance. The war, it sucked the youth out of all of us."

"Some guys I knew wanted to die there," Woody said. "I mean, their friends were there, they'd died there . . ."

Had that been Woody's wish? Kate wondered.

Bernie said, "The Vietcong were boys too, except the average twenty-year-old looked like he was anywhere from forty to sixty years old."

"They were very, very vicious fighters, Bernie." The stridency had left Melanie's tone. "Even the women. My Lai, the Calley trial, maybe what those soldiers did was wrong, but I could understand it."

"I couldn't," Bernie said. "But the thing was, Melanie, there weren't any happy endings for anybody. Any soldier I helped fix up, I knew he'd have to go back and get shot at all over again."

"Dacey, you're pretty quiet about all this," Melanie said. "Cat got your tongue?"

He shrugged. "A buddy went back to the World before I did, he wrote me. How he went to the VA, and here's how much they think of what he's done in Nam—they send him to some factory paying minimum wage. So he goes to UPS, I think it was, and gets on their waiting list. Same for the post office, the phone company, you name it. His grateful country finally lets him have a job in a Wrigley Field hot dog stand. So I came back knowing some of the score."

Rachel said, "Stuff like that was why I married Michael. It's why vets ended up marrying each other, or just drifted around like lost souls for a long time, like Allan did."

"A lot of vets are okay, you know," Martin said. "Have good jobs, die of natural causes."

"Spoken like a man who took his ROTC at Harvard," Doc quipped. "But you're right, Martin. Of course you're right."

"Yeah, most of us in this room look to be pretty okay," Melanie said.

After an incredulous blink at Melanie's statement,

Kate said, "I understand this was Allan's first reunion. Anybody have any reason why?"

Melanie examined her fingernails. "I'm not saying this was a big reason or anything, but he was real interested to know you were coming, Kate."

If she's blaming me for his death—

"I'll fess up," Rachel said. "Kate and Allan finally turning up is a reason I'm here."

"Me too," Dacey said. "I really wanted to reconnect."

"And me," Gabe said.

Consigning her suspicion of Melanie's motives to the realm of paranoia, Kate smiled at Rachel, Dacey, and Gabe. Rachel's remark she could understand—they had considerable shared history. But she had never understood Gabe and Dacey's affection for her, or why they had remained in intermittent touch with her over the years.

Doc said abruptly, "Why are you here, Martin?"

Martin fussed with the cuffs of his cashmere sweater, rolling them up as he replied, "I'm not quite sure how to answer that, Edward. I didn't have any perspective back then, except hating that I had to be there. I did my surgery, it was brutal, intense, desperate, sometimes I had to work fourteen, eighteen hours. But as appalling as it was, afterward I could get out of there. On days when I didn't have any surgery, I made my rounds and left again. I knew the nurses were the real heroes in the trenches. You're right, Woody, I was a mechanic making bodies war-worthy again. I knew it then, I knew it. I never felt . . . a real part of anything . . . valuable."

Woody mumbled, "Don't mind me, I'm just so god-damn . . ." He gestured helplessly.

Identifying strongly with Martin's words, Kate was shocked that he had spoken them. Unlike any other person in this room, even Melanie, she had not been required to do any of the grisly or dangerous tasks of the war, only to funnel supplies to those who did. But her military service had been considered an asset by the law enforcement agencies to which she had applied. Never had she dreamed that Martin would feel the same inferiority she did. She asked him, "And you feel differently now?"

"Whether I wanted to be in Vietnam or not, I was there. I did my work, it was important to do it, and to be there. I guess I finally started to feel comfortable about having earned my way here with the rest of you."

Melanie looked stunned by what she had heard. "Good God, how could you—*lots* of our guys wouldn't have made it back except for you and Doc."

Doc said, nodding at Martin, "Saving somebody didn't seem to do all that much good, Melanie. I saved soldiers injured beyond recovery and sent their broken bodies and minds home. And if they weren't broken, then I sent them back into the abyss they'd come out of. We saved little Horatio—only to present him with a life as an orphan and a beggar."

Kate said gently, "Doc, this is why you quit."

"Oh no, Kate," he said with a brief, arid chuckle, "I'm not nearly that noble. I quit because I couldn't be a surgeon anymore, and believe me I tried practicing every other kind of medicine, I really tried, but I couldn't do that, either. I was fine for about five or six years after I got back and then suddenly I couldn't pick up a scalpel without having flashbacks."

Kate understood in profound anguish that she could do nothing to alleviate the naked pain she saw in his face; she could provide him with none of the comfort and healing he had once conferred upon her.

He said, "I'd gown up to operate, and I'd be back in the 95th Evac and there'd be all these mortar wounds—gaping chests and bellies, shattered limbs to amputate. I couldn't keep my hands from shaking. I haven't been able to since."

"Doc," Kate said huskily, "nobility is exactly why you had to quit. Why was it important to you that Allan know?"

"Allan was the first one to tell me the war was total bullshit. I called him a traitor. I needed to say my mea culpas."

"You didn't have to tell him. He knew," Rachel said.

Doc couldn't be a killer, Kate thought, he couldn't be.

Martin said, "I've never forgotten how incredibly stoic our Marines were, and how it seemed they always died on us at night. Every night you knew the family of some nineteen- or twenty-year-old kid would be getting a visit from the Marine Corps two days later."

Martin pushed up the sleeves of his sweater, cleared his throat. "Speaking of amputations, Doc," he said with a shadow of a smile, "after you left I did a lot of circumcisions. I found out the guys would get a couple of weeks off for that."

Watching Aimee again wipe her eyes with a tissue, Kate was thinking that beyond herself it was doubtful that the Marine Corps had made a bereavement visit to anyone in the U.S. when Cap had been reported missing in action—he had no immediate family. She wondered if any of those distant relatives in Tennessee had heard of, or taken note of, his disappearance.

"In one way or another you were always saying goodbye," Rachel said. "Even now it's hard for me to get that close to anybody. I don't invest any more in people than I have to because it's like being in Nam—"

"Yeah," Bernie said, "you'd get close to somebody over there and all of a sudden it was time to DEROS."

"Date of expected return from overseas," Rachel explained to Aimee. "The day everybody began dreaming of the minute you set foot in Nam."

Kate was snared by a fold in the ribbon of time. All her own good-byes lined up in painful array, and she realized that Cap had been only one of many losses. Beginning with Bernie's return to the World, followed closely by Dacey. Cap . . . then Gabe, and Rachel. Even Melanie had been a loss. Only Doc, Woody, and Martin had lasted the length of her tour.

Bernie was saying, "Here I was, geared up from having all this responsibility for human life, then I go back to civilian life and I can't even start an IV without supervision. To this day I still want to scream that they should have seen my skills when lives were on the line."

"Two doctors I know came back morphine addicts," Doc said.

"Hell, I knew a dozen nurses who went home hooked on something or other," Bernie said.

"I was hooked on adrenaline," Melanie said. "I had, like, twelve to fourteen jobs in fourteen or fifteen years. Everything since seems like . . . horseshit.''

"All the drinking," Kate said to Bernie, "it was really something, wasn't it? For somebody like me who didn't drink much before she got there."

Bernie said, "I don't remember ever being drunk, but off duty I always had a drink in my hand, you know."

"I got marijuana right off the streets from the mamasans, already rolled," Melanie said. "Everybody was on something," she added.

"Gabe," Dacey said, "remember Jimbo?"

"Sure."

"He never could understand how come Will Maloney needed so many emergency flight packs. But each one of those babies held eight government-issued tabs of the purest methamphetamine you could find anywhere. Got me through chauffeuring the big shots around."

"Dacey," Kate said, "how did you feel about Cap turning in that report on you guys?"

"What report?"

"About the water buffalo."

"The water—oh, that." He waved a hand. "No skin off my ass. But Will was really pissed."

Kate kept her face carefully blank. Dacey's answer was too glib, had been given too casually. And was patently untrue. There had been hell to pay over the shooting of that water buffalo, and Dacey had been in the middle of it.

"Will sure as hell was pissed," Woody said. "But nowhere near as pissed as you and Gabe over all those rumors about Cap." He laughed raucously.

Dacey's eyes narrowed. "Yeah, well..." As he paused, Kate caught the covert glance he flicked her way. "All I cared about was not getting fragged some night by a freak looking to clean up the world to his own taste."

"The same thing crossed my mind," Gabe said.

Kate kept her tone neutral. "You're saying both of you were good friends of Cap, so when you found out he was gay you figured everybody thought you were too."

"You got it," Gabe said.

"Well, you guys were right," Bernie said with a laugh, raising her glass to them. "Everybody wondering if you were a nest of gay boys made for a lot better gossip than the colonel and his hooch girl."

"Jesus," Gabe said.

"Nobody cared," Doc said.

"Hmmph," Dacey muttered, and drew on his cigarette.

"There were lots of gays over there," Melanie said. "Everybody thought Cap was the best guy on earth."

Doc said, "I thought about Cap during that whole gays-in-the-military fiasco, and this year too when the gays marched in New York for the twenty-fifth anniversary of that civil rights riot..." He made a circling signal with his hand, looking from Kate to Aimee for one of them to fill in the blank.

"The Stonewall Inn in Greenwich Village," Aimee supplied.

Doc nodded. "Yes. Here all of us were in Vietnam that very same year, serving in the name of everything this country stands for—and we come home to find out none of it mattered. It didn't matter how heroic our conduct was, how many medals anybody won, our country had turned its back on us. So we end up keeping that whole part of our life a secret. Just like the gays. It took us a long time to get together and recognize our right to be angry and bitter as hell at our country, just like it did for—"

"What *is* this shit?" snarled Woody.

Bernie said thoughtfully, "Doc, there really are a lot of similarities between—"

"I for one don't care for the comparison," Melanie said. "They're two very different . . . things."

Kate glanced at Aimee; her struggle to remain silent was visible in the tension of her body.

Martin said, "Anybody who did throw a fit over Cap being gay, you could lay money he was a lifer."

Admiring Martin's smooth sidetracking of the topic, Kate also saw Gabe and Dacey exchange a glance.

"Lifers," Rachel said, shaking her head. "The best kind of people you'd ever want to know, they could make you so glad they're looking after the country— but always that small group of them who never want anything to change. They make life a misery, they do it to this very day." She mimicked a gruff male voice: "Only two ways to do anything—the Marine Corps way and the wrong way."

"You got that right," muttered Gabe. "God, country, and the Marine Corps."

"And not necessarily in that order," Martin said. "You couldn't have an intelligent conversation with any of those people, there wasn't an issue they couldn't oversimplify."

"I'm a live-and-let-live guy," Woody said. "I got nothing against gays, but anybody spread those kind of rumors about me I'd of carved their nuts off."

"Woody," Rachel said good-naturedly, "there isn't a gay man I know who'd look twice at you."

"That means a lot coming from you, Miss Nightingale," Woody said. "Everybody knew about you and Kate."

"We did?" inquired Melanie.

Nonplussed, Kate uttered, "Knew what?"

"You damn women all stick together," Woody said, dismissing her with a wave. "You two"—he pointed at Kate—"if you weren't boozing it up with the rest of us you were in Miss Nightingale's hooch. Miss Nightingale sure as shit wasn't interested in anybody's dick over there."

"At least not yours, apparently," suggested Doc.

Kate started to speak, subsided as Rachel said flatly, "I was too tired."

Dacey said, "So we can put it in the paper, Rachel— you're heterosexual."

Slumped in her chair, lank black hair falling over her face, Bernie grunted, "Who cares," and downed her bourbon.

Rachel was smiling at Dacey. "Healing, Dacey, what a profession. Everybody needs it, most men aren't good at giving it, not even doctors sometimes when it comes to emotional healing. In Nam, all Kate had to do was walk into the room and I felt better. She was the healthiest of any of us."

"That's a fact," Bernie said.

"I think all of us felt that way," Gabe said.

Kate absorbed these statements with astonishment. "You never told me—"

Rachel said, "We didn't tell each other a lot of things, Kate."

"You didn't answer the question, Rach," Dacey said.

"Didn't I," she said indifferently.

"I really liked Cap and let me tell you the worst part," Woody said. "When the adjutant told him his orders came through for the Third Division, Gabe got right on the horn to Allan, remember? Allan told us he'd look out for him, remember, Gabe?"

"Sure I remember," Gabe said with a trace of irritation.

"If Cap's platoon'd been anywhere near Allan's, they'd of found him or they'd still be out there looking. The one thing Allan agreed with the Marine Corps about was never leave your wounded behind. He would of called in supplies and kept those men out there killing VC till they found Cap or died trying. Allan was a real one."

"A good leader," Doc interpreted for Aimee.

"The best," Woody confirmed fervently.

Kate was smiling at Woody. "I remember now what you had written on your helmet. Red Death."

He said defensively, "Hey, I really believed in what we were doing over there."

"I know you did, Woody. I did too."

"All the Nam vets went over there believing in it," Melanie said.

Having observed Gabe shaking his head during Woody's remarks about Cap, Aimee ventured, "Gabe, what do you think happened to Cap?"

She caught Kate's eye and was astonished by the
flash of gratitude before Kate's face closed up again.
Not much wonder she's being so quiet—she can't be
a detective here, Aimee realized. She desperately wants
to be one but she can't.

"I don't think it ever mattered about Allan looking
out for him," Gabe said. "I think Cap walked away.
Got up there to the DMZ and figured his chances of
being greased were about the same as the sun coming
up tomorrow, so he went out on his first patrol, got
himself separated from his platoon, and kept right on
walking."

Aimee saw nods, heard murmurs of assent from
around the room. She asked, "Because he was gay?"

"Maybe that," Martin said, "more likely because he
was at a FEBA—the forward edge of a battle area.
Where most guys get shot."

Doc said, "I'm betting he met up with Allan, and
being smarter than me, he let himself hear what Allan
said about the war."

Kate said, nodding, "He knew it already, Doc."

Aimee asked, "How would he get out?"

Gabe said, "Cap wasn't some GI Joe, he was a lieutenant. My guess is, he hitched a ride on a chopper.
Found one leaving to pick up supplies somewhere, and
smooth-talked his way on board. The chopper pilots
were great about taking you if there was room, all of
us rode one at one time or another, flew all around
the countryside."

"That's right," Kate said.

Melanie nodded. "It's how I got all over the place.
Let me tell you, sometimes it was a lot easier getting a

ride into some places than it was getting out."

"Gabe did it all the time," Rachel said affectionately. "Remember, Mr. Cumshaw Operator?"

"Sure do, Rachel," he said with a grin.

"This cumshaw business," Melanie said. "Did you get rich out of it, Gabe?"

"No cumshaw operator ever did," Gabe said indignantly. "It was pure barter."

"Gabe was our miracle man," Rachel told Aimee. "One time the air conditioner blew in one of the wards. Going through Kate and Supply Command meant req forms in triplicate and finding out a month later the standard air conditioner wasn't in stock, but they had another kind and you could order it by filling out another form—"

Chuckling, Kate said, "Gabe got it in a day—traded an enemy rifle to another Division for one."

"Cumshaw—I've never even heard the word," Aimee said.

"Chinese, I think," Gabe said. "Anything you had you could trade. Enemy rifles and bottles of Canadian Club or Seagram's could get you anything on earth. But it was only about food and equipment, never money," he added, looking resentfully at Melanie.

Melanie said, "You're telling us you got nothing out of it."

"Worship," Bernie said, chuckling. "Anything we really needed, we threw ourselves at Gabe's feet."

Melanie said, "Well, you'd have had to steal a lot to match the Vietnamese and their black markets—"

"Gabe," Aimee said doggedly, "assuming Cap could

get away from where he was, how would he get out of the country?"

But it was Dacey who answered. "That would be the hard part," he offered, his gaze connecting directly with her. "He could get himself to the Laotian border easy enough—Khe Sanh is real close to Laos. Anything could happen to him there, maybe that's when he came up missing. Hell, maybe he's even living there. These days, nobody's looking for POWs or MIAs in places like Laos or Cambodia, not like they're scouring Vietnam."

"Today they're looking everywhere," Kate said in contradiction.

"Yeah," Gabe said. "Who could ever guess there'd be this kind of attention to our MIAs. Everybody spits in our faces back then, now they're looking for our people under every twig."

"You got that right," Dacey said.

Aimee gazed at Dacey in sympathy.

Martin said, "I read somewhere we've spent around three million dollars per man searching for our people over there. And we've got veterans, poor torn-up devils just wandering the streets of our own country and they're MIAs in their own right."

"Hear, hear," Rachel murmured.

Aimee wondered what else she should ask to help Kate. How could she draw people out? "I know four of you are in the medical profession one way or the other. And Gabe's with a bartering company and Melanie's a restaurant hostess. Dacey and Woody—what about you?"

Woody said, "I run an auto body shop."

"Into the ground, from what I hear," Dacey joked. "I own twenty-eight franchise Econo Cleaners throughout Kentucky and Tennessee."

"Nice going, Woody, Dacey," Kate said, nodding. "Everybody here seems to be doing okay. What about Allan, what did he do?"

"He was a crop duster," Melanie said with a giggle.

"Once a shit-bird, always a shit-bird," Woody said.

"I truly wish I could have met him," Aimee said.

"We shook hands when he checked in," Gabe said mournfully, "promised we'd catch up later. Who'd have guessed . . ."

"Me too," Woody said. "Saw him in the hallway, asked him to drop into my room for a drink."

"Nobody else saw him before the party?"

"I thought Kate was the detective," Melanie said.

"I'm sorry to intrude—I know he meant a lot to all of you. But Kate and I get shot at and then this man dies . . ."

"Melanie," said a bleary-eyed Bernie, "whyn't you stop being a bisch."

Melanie said, not unkindly, "I was born a bitch, Bernie. And I think you need to get to bed, sleep it off."

"I think we all do," Dacey said, getting up and lifting his chair up and away from the window. "It's getting on for one o'clock." He smiled at Aimee. "Some of us need our beauty sleep."

Aimee smiled back at him, feeling a current of connection between them and thinking that of all the people she had met, he seemed the one she could perhaps talk to. Maybe, on her own, she could gather some useful information.

As Rachel stood up, stretched, then helped Bernie to her wobbly feet, Melanie asked in alarm, "Hey, hey, what's going on here?"

"How about we grab a cup of coffee together sometime tomorrow morning?" Aimee asked Dacey amid the scraping back of chairs and the general hubbub of leave-taking.

Dacey said with enthusiasm, "Great, I'd like that."

"The night's just started," Melanie wailed. "I came a long way to see you guys again. What's happened to all you party animals?"

"We grew up," Martin said, pushing back from the table. He held a hand out to Doc, pulling him up from the sofa. Plucking at Doc's baseball shirt, Martin added, "Or at least some of us did."

"Don't get too carried away with this growing up business, Martin," Doc said, and punched him lightly on the biceps.

13

"**R**OUGH night," Jill Manners said. She was escorting Kate, striding slightly in front of her along the fourth floor hallway to the elevator that led to the parking lot in the rear of the Inn.

"For all of us," Kate said. "You've been on duty how many hours?" Jill looked remarkably fresh, her posture erect, her uniform as crisp as when Kate had last seen her.

A hand preventing the elevator door from closing, Jill followed Kate into the elevator. "I have a personal interest in this case," she said.

"I appreciate it," Kate said. "I hope I can return the favor."

"I hope you can't," Jill joked. "When you're finished with Carver and Duffy, get a good night's sleep, Kate. Your room is under surveillance."

Kate took Jill's hand in wordless thanks. Jill's dark eyes met hers in an unguarded warmth of communication as her cool hand pressed firmly on Kate's, squeezed, released. Kate thought not for the first time that lesbians were among the most beautiful women on earth.

Just outside the rear door to the Inn, their faces

looking jaundiced in the greenish-yellow illumination from a single light standard, Carver and Duffy waited in a tan-colored Chevrolet Caprice crisscrossed by striations of pouring rain. Neither the lateness of the hour nor the foul weather, Kate noted, had convinced Carver to so much as loosen his tie. Duffy, on the other hand, looked as rumpled as she felt.

She tossed her shoulder bag into the backseat of the car and climbed quickly in after it; Carver drove out of the lot, windshield wipers rapidly thunking. She welcomed the warmth of the car; the brief exposure to the wet frigid night had chilled her.

Carver parked less than a block away, under a streetlight, but turned off only the windshield wipers. Both detectives turned to her in the backseat, Duffy with notebook in hand.

"Fucking rain's never gonna end," Duffy said, dabbing a neatly folded handkerchief at his nose. Kate could smell mint on his breath.

"If it does, winter's next," Carver said indifferently. "Kate, check-in time for everybody at the reunion— they were all here before your room got shot up. Except for the victim."

Brushing rain from her jacket, Kate nodded. "I'm not sure it matters anymore."

"How so?" Duffy asked. "Whatcha got for us?"

"A theory. Based on two facts. I never met Allan Gerlock, and Cap didn't either—until he went up to the DMZ. I think Gerlock was murdered to prevent him from meeting me."

As if aware that his incredulity showed, Carver quickly nodded. "Okay, go on."

"The shots fired into my room were aimed too high to hit anybody—I don't think it had anything to do with somebody not wanting to be a cop-killer, I think it was meant to chase me out of town." Smiling ruefully, she added, "It would've worked too, except for my stubborn partner—I was all set to pack up and get out. Not to mention I didn't want to be here in the first place. I think this killer was clearly reluctant to kill me."

"Kate," Carver said, "I'm not saying I disagree with your theory, but all these people look squeaky-clean—nothing's come up from NCIC or anywhere else except on Dacey, and his sheet's just like he said, sixties stuff, all B and E's. He came out of the Marine Corps a solid citizen with his burglary habit cured."

The heated car held the earthen odor of damp wool, a smell Kate remembered from wintertime school cloakrooms of her childhood. "I'm convinced the key to this whole thing is that somebody got to Allan Gerlock—who came here alone—and killed him to prevent him from meeting me." She raised her voice as the rain picked up, drumming a tattoo on the car roof. "Carver, Duffy, I need you to tell me what you found in Allan Gerlock's room about Cap Pearson."

"Gerlock wrote the letters C.A.P. as he was dying," Duffy said.

The explosion she was expecting from Carver did not materialize. He said evenly, "The initials were inscribed on the bathroom floor in blood under Gerlock's right palm."

She was silent for the few moments that would be expected of her to digest such news. "Thank you," she finally said, nodding. "This whole train of thought started with Dacey and Martin Goldberg speculating about Cap. I loved the Cap Pearson I knew twenty-five years ago, he was the finest man I knew next to my own father. I could never believe he was dead—not without proof. All these years later I think I may have been absolutely right in that belief."

Dimly she realized how affected she had been by the events of the evening; the words had tumbled out of her without the usual self-censorship. "The man I knew back then could never have cut someone's throat. But something must have happened to make him into a man I no longer know—"

Duffy interrupted. "What exactly did Dacey and the doctor tell you to make you so sure the man's alive?"

She was glad for the interruption; self-censorship was a virtue when emotion began to run away from you. "Dacey mentioned how easy it would be for Cap to board a helicopter at Khe Sanh and get himself to the Laotian border. Dacey thinks he might have vanished in Laos, or maybe he's still living over there. But Martin's comment got me really thinking. He said we've got veterans wandering the streets of our own country and they're MIAs in their own right."

"I don't get it," Duffy said.

"I think I do," Carver said. "Keep talking."

"If Allan Gerlock named his killer, I think we ought to take him at his word. I think you should run the name Charles A. Pearson through every database you have. His social security number, all his vital stats—you might be able to get them faster through the Defense Intelligence Agency than the Marine Corps. The DIA's a branch of the Department of Defense responsible for sightings of MIAs.''

Both Carver and Duffy looked astonished. "How on earth would you know a fact like that?" Carver demanded.

She knew she had to smile to deflect their sympathy, but the smile felt painful. "All these years I felt in a sense I was family to Cap, so I . . . kept up with the activity about our MIAs.''

The smile obviously didn't work; Carver and Duffy gazed at her with a compassion that made her writhe, Carver rubbing his chin as if trying to scrub off his five-o'clock shadow as he contemplated her.

She said, "Maybe you've got some connections—"

"After twenty years in this town I have connections to connections, even on a Sunday," Carver said. "If there's a link, we'll try our damnedest to find some answers before all of you leave.''

Duffy nodded. "We have surveillance on your room tonight.''

"Jill Manners told me—I'm grateful. If Cap Pearson is alive, I suspect I don't need it. If he killed Allan Gerlock, either he got in and out of the hotel without being observed, or he altered his appearance—pretty easy after all these years. David Olson of course wouldn't know him from a pile of sand.''

"I have one very big problem with your theory," Carver said.

"Me too," Duffy said. "Why the hell would this guy have to kill Gerlock so the two of you wouldn't meet?"

Weariness permeated her, as if the effects of all her caffeine intake had suddenly evaporated. "The answer

has to be something Allan Gerlock knew about Cap
and his past or his present life. Something about Cap
that would come out if we met."

"Yeah? Like what?" Duffy challenged her. "Drug
running? International white slavery? Child pornogra-
phy? What would any of that have to do with you?"

She closed her eyes. "I don't know." She said bitterly, "We may never find out all the answers. If I'm
right about this, if Cap's alive, he's had twenty-five
years of perfecting his disappearing act."

"All I know is, it sounds crazy as hell," Carver said.

"No crazier than the guy last week who stabbed his
wife to death for buying Crest instead of Colgate toothpaste," Duffy said.

"Kate, I'm willing to give your theory some cre-
dence," Carver said. "But Duffy and I, we've expanded
beyond the group that's here this weekend to Gerlock's present life. He's from Ohio—we've got the Co-
lumbus PD looking into things back there."

She nodded; she would have done exactly the same
thing.

"Maybe the shooting into your room and this murder are actually not related," Duffy said. "Maybe this'll
all come down to a girlfriend with a beef or somebody
collecting an unpaid debt. The thing is, David Olson's
our only eyewitness about who came in and out of the
Inn."

"True." No one knew better than she did that the
credibility of an eyewitness could range anywhere on
the scale of reliability from zero to ten. But in her
mind, David Olson ranked as a ten. "I respectfully disagree—I do think we've been right all along about the

shooting and this murder being connected."

"Your theory at this point has just as much weight as anyone else's," Carver said amiably, switching on the windshield wipers and putting the car in gear.

Watching the rain sluice down the windshield, Kate felt weighed down by her weariness. "Whoever killed Allan Gerlock didn't want to kill me—that's the bottom-line reason I think it could be Cap. No matter how much he might have changed over twenty-five years, I can't believe he could bring himself to kill me."

Carver pulled into the parking lot. "Regardless of any theory, we're keeping you under surveillance at least through the night, Detective," he said. "You be careful."

14

WAITING for Kate's return, Aimee lay in bed numbly watching shafts of rain shatter furiously on the window. She had long since closed the bedroom louvers that so many hours ago—an eon ago, it seemed—had gained her entry into Kate's past.

The door of the suite opened; moments later Kate quietly entered the bedroom. She came over to the bed and stood there, uncertainty in her face. "After what you've heard tonight, I guess you've got a few questions about a few things," she said.

Touched by the sadness in her face, the weariness in her voice, Aimee propped herself up on an elbow. "I've got a lot more explanations than questions." She gestured toward the living room of the suite. "I felt like a child in that room tonight, I didn't belong there. I went blundering into your past like a fool, Kate. I *am* a fool. I had absolutely no right to force you to come here, it's my fault all this—"

"Stop that. *Nothing* about this murder is your fault. And coming here's . . . actually it's had its good points." Kate lowered her shoulder bag beside the bed and stripped off her jacket and sweatshirt.

Aimee was going to ask what those good points

might be, but said instead, "I understand now—sometimes it simply costs too much to remember."

"I'm grateful you understand that. But you're no child, you have your own wisdom. The festering from that year over there—it needed to be exposed, I needed to face it—"

"Kate, it's so ironic. You went over there an outcast and came home less of an outcast—your military service was an asset to you, it gave you a career. They went over there as standard issue Americans and came home outcasts."

"I guess that's true, but you can see . . . compared to the rest of them I didn't do much of anything over there."

Aimee bolted up to a sitting position. "That's absolutely crazy. And absolutely *typical* of you." Again she gestured toward the suite's living room. "Didn't you hear how much they think of you? Three of those people came here because they knew you'd be here. Didn't you hear what they said? You kept them sane. You—"

"Aimee, they risked their lives and their sanity. I didn't."

Exasperated, she snapped, "For the life of me I've never understood this frontline mentality business, this idea that you have to risk your damn life to be worth anything. And you've felt guilty about this for twenty-five years. Haven't you," she demanded, when Kate did not speak.

"Yes," Kate said.

"It's why you came home and became a cop. Because by your lights you didn't do enough over there."

Kate's eyes widened as if she were perceiving this possibility for the very first time. "I guess . . . that might have been part of it."

"How much longer are you going to carry this stupid, ridiculous, *unnecessary* guilt?"

Kate smiled then. "Maybe not much longer. I love you, Aimee. I love you most of all for the way you see me."

"I love you too, and what I love is what I see. And what I see is how you are." Aimee lay back down on the bed. "If that's not too complicated."

"I'll try to work with it," Kate said.

A few minutes later Kate came out of the bathroom wearing a dark blue LAPD T-shirt. Again watching the rain patterns on the window, Aimee asked, "What was your place, uh, your . . . Quonset hut like over there?"

Kate sat on the bed. She touched Aimee's face, her hand stroking gently down her cheek and neck, and across her bare shoulders. "What was it like where I lived, you mean? Basic. Plywood walls blow-torched to dark brown. A cot, footlocker, regular locker, dresser, small refrigerator, small stereo. And a beautiful Vietnamese room divider carved from bamboo."

At the shadow that passed across Kate's eyes, Aimee guessed that the room divider had been a gift. From Cap?

"Will you be warm enough without this?" Aimee murmured, sliding her hands under Kate's T-shirt.

"If you promise to help."

Aimee slid the T-shirt over Kate's head, pulled Kate down under the covers and into her arms, tucked Kate's head onto her shoulder, warming Kate's cool body with her own. She slid her hands over the smooth wide breadth of Kate's back, then up into her hair, feeling Kate shudder, not from pleasure but like a taut string vibrating from touch.

Knowing this had to have been one of the hardest days of Kate's life, she asked softly, "What did you get sick from over there?"

"FUO. Fever of unknown origin." Kate's voice was just above a whisper. "The war was about last on the list of what could land you in a hospital. Lots of us came down with things like malaria and typhus. I was sick for about a week, deathly sick for two days."

"Rachel nursed you."

Kate turned her face in toward Aimee's throat. "Yes." The word was a puff of warmth against Aimee's skin.

"I'm glad she did. Were you in love with her?"

She could feel Kate tense, then, another puff of warmth: "Yes."

"I would have been too," Aimee said. "I'll bet a lot of people were in love with her."

"Everybody, I think." Kate's head angled up and she spoke in a more audible voice. "Everybody. Those two days, I was conscious off and on. I was with eighteen- and nineteen-year-old boys with pieces of their bodies missing . . . I could hear moaning and crying, I knew I was there because I was dying too, or I'd be crippled somehow like them . . . Being in that bed for forty-eight hours was so terrifying, except for Rachel. All she had to do was touch my face . . ."

"I'm glad she was there—I'm not just talking about the hospital. Whatever the two of you had together."

The long sighing from Kate seemed to deflate her body. "She needed to . . . keep everything for herself."

Aimee remembered Rachel's words of less than an hour ago: *In one way or another you were always saying good-bye. Even now it's hard for me to get that close to anybody. I don't invest any more in people than I have to because it's like being in Nam——*"

"I think she still does," Aimee said.

"I was never quite sure," Kate said, "do you even think she's a lesbian?"

"I think it doesn't matter," she answered Kate quietly. "I'm glad she was there. I'm glad Rachel and Bernie both were there. They're born nurses, born healers, they . . . ." She groped for a word. "They *burn* with it."

Aimee pressed her face into Kate's hair, the thought fleeting through her that the grayer Kate's hair became, the softer it seemed to be.

"I've been lucky, Aimee, so very lucky about the women in my life."

"Cap—"

Again Kate tensed against her. "I can't . . . I'll talk about him sometime, I promise you. Just not now."

"Tell me whatever you want to, but I know you loved him too." She would let Kate assume that Bernie or someone else from the group had told her about him.

She stroked Kate's body, her hands moving slowly, as if her palms and fingers could spread balm. Desire spread through her in a thick, slow-moving, familiar tide. Desire for Kate was always in her, increasing and receding, but ever-present, a hunger beginning its rise immediately after satiation. Constant desire, rooted not in physical factors or age difference—Kate's hungers more than matched hers—but in a constant wanting to traverse the landscape of Kate that she could only enter and explore through lovemaking.

Tonight she had found a new avenue into this woman who believed she must hide her pain and give only her love.

She tightened her arms as the curves of Kate's body sought hers in a warmth that was almost liquid, and she felt the tremors in Kate's body that signified relaxation into deep sleep.

She kissed Kate's forehead and heard a sleepy murmur in response. If she had found another key into Kate, it was into the same landscape, and she could traverse it with only the greatest trepidation—and, like their lovemaking, with the greatest tenderness.

15

GLANCING at the gray-filled window, then at the bedside clock, Kate eased Aimee's arm from around her and slid from the bed. Aimee muttered in her sleep and then turned onto her stomach, pulling the covers up over her shoulder and the pillow further down under her head. Kate moved over to the window.

At 8:15 this Sunday morning light traffic moved rapidly past the Inn; a few people strolled by under umbrellas in the light drizzle. Only one squad car was visible, parked inconspicuously down the street. Apparently the coroner's van had come and gone during the night, taking Allan Gerlock's body away for autopsy.

Cap.

Remembering the night before, a mantle of depression settling over her shoulders, she walked into the bathroom, into the shower.

When she emerged, Aimee was sitting up in bed, rubbing her eyes and yawning. "Morning, honey," she said. "What's the agenda today?"

A towel wrapped around her, Kate leaned down, kissed her on the temple. "I'm sure we'll hear from the police before too long," she answered. "Beyond that, I'm not sure." A call to Torrie Holden would need to wait until at least ten o'clock to allow for the time difference.

"Now that you've slept on this, what do you think?" Aimee asked.

Now that she had slept on it, and with her body and mind reenergized by the shower, she was vexed by uncertainties. No longer did she feel the same confidence in the theory she had advanced to Carver and Duffy. Last night in her physical and emotional exhaustion it had been too easy to explain away motive by conceding that they might never know the exact reason why Allan Gerlock had been murdered.

A key piece was floating loose, something that she hadn't figured into the puzzle of this murder; she could feel it, almost grasp it. Something she had learned last night, something that would give her an inroad toward the truth of this man.

"Tell me what *you* think," she told Aimee. "I really want to know."

Aimee said promptly, "Cross off Rachel and Bernie and Doc. People who give their souls trying to save other people's lives aren't going to turn around and take one."

Kate smiled. "What about Martin?"

Aimee shook her hair out, combing tangles with her fingers. "I know he's a doctor, honey, and a nice man, but I get the feeling he could just as easily be a stockbroker or a college professor. Or anything."

Kate nodded. "Tell me more."

"My sense is Gabe wouldn't do this, but I also know that's crazy. He was a Marine and God knows how many people he killed over there and he could do it again. I think Dacey and Woody could use any kind of rationale to kill somebody. I think Melanie could kill somebody and sit down to a full-course dinner with the body in the same room. Now, what do you think?''

Kate was chuckling. "Aimee, any one of them could kill."

"You have to think that way, you're a cop. Anyway, hold the thought.'' Aimee got up and headed for the bathroom.

Wondering if the sun would ever again shine on this dismal city, Kate donned jeans and a denim shirt, strapped on her shoulder holster and zipped up a windbreaker to conceal the weapon. Aimee's words nagged at her, increasing the feeling that in the scenario she had described for Carver and Duffy she had badly misread something.

She called in to Aimee, "Be back in a minute, I want to check things out."

"You be careful."

"I will. Aimee, don't answer the door. I mean it. To anyone, for any reason. Got that?"

"Got it."

She didn't trust Aimee's sense of caution for a New York minute. Sighing, she eased open the door and peered out into the hallway. Empty. So much for surveillance. Edging out, she let the door swing shut behind her. The doors along this hallway were closed, but, she noted, unlike the first floor they were slightly recessed, and one of them could be slightly ajar. A hand at the opening to her jacket, she moved slowly and cautiously down the hallway to the elevator and pushed the button. Glancing around, shoulder blades prickling, she listened to it complain its way toward her. Getting herself and Aimee out of this town couldn't happen soon enough.

In the lobby, a single cop, a stranger to her, eyed her briefly from where he sat in an armchair, then returned to his Sunday *Post.* A desk clerk she did not know was checking out four guests, one of them John Stafford, his tall frame handsomely clad in a heavy, cocoa-brown Nike sweat suit. He broke out of his place in line to come over to her and shake her hand.

"Good luck to you, Mr. Stafford," she said.

"Good luck to *you*," he said with a rich chuckle. "From everything that's gone on here, it would appear you're the one that needs it."

"It would appear," she answered with a grin.

The staircase door into the lobby opened, and David Olson, looking pale, adjusting his bow tie over a wilted-looking white shirt, came into the lobby, surveying it as if expecting to find damage. She countered his offer of an unsmiling nod with a nod of her own, plus a smile. With Allan Gerlock's body on the premises until the early hours of the morning Olson would have stayed at the hotel overnight, she guessed.

As for Carver and Duffy, if they had followed anything close to what her routine would be, they would have finished up here, gone to the station and entered their preliminary reports, gone home to grab a few hours of sleep and a shave, and were probably on their way back here now to pick up the strands of this case.

Kate looked through the doorway of the Patriot Room. At a corner table in the sparsely populated res-

taurant, Rachel and Martin and Doc and his wife sat
drinking coffee. Bernie and her Ralphie were probably
occupied nursing Bernie through her hangover. And
Gabe, Melanie, and Dacey could be sleeping in, or
even having breakfast together off the premises. In
many respects, the Inn on Liberty Square seemed to
be returning to normal.

Rachel spotted her, waved; Doc beckoned to her. As
Kate made her way over to the table, she noted with
amusement that this morning Doc had donned a pair
of gray overalls over a red flannel shirt, along with a
train engineer's gray cap.

"We've only just ordered—you and Aimee come and
have breakfast with us," Martin invited.

"I'd love to." She was famished. "I'll go get Aimee."

"The fellow on the desk mentioned that Dacey's
checked out," Doc said.

"Really," Kate said, halting to digest this news.

Martin said, "What do you think, Kate, did he check
out—or run?"

"Why on earth would he run?" Rachel said, her
hands circling her coffee cup, her face looking tired.
"Dacey never even met Allan."

"True," Kate said thoughtfully. "See you in a few
minutes."

In the lobby, she again exchanged nods with David
Olson, then went over to the desk and said to the
plump young man who was working with David Olson,
"I understand that Dacey—" Dammit, she still didn't
know Dacey's first name. "I understand that Mr. Dacey
checked out this morning."

"He did indeed," the desk clerk answered in a musical tenor voice.

"What time was that?"

"Around six."

"Thank you."

Turning away she looked at the uniformed cop in the lobby in disgust. He was paying no attention whatever, he was far more interested in his Sunday paper. Why weren't Carver and Duffy here? Or Jill?

As she made her way toward the elevator, her annoyance faded; the sheer normality of the Inn, and the light of day, however grayish, were too comforting.

Dacey. Kate reviewed what she knew about Dacey—which was not very much, she conceded. Cap had never named any of his sexual liaisons in Vietnam, part of the protective behavior some gay people adopted in the military—what you didn't know you couldn't accidentally or deliberately reveal. But he had talked enough about the physical attributes of one battle-hardened ultra-macho Marine in particular that she had thought she had pieced together sufficient description to recognize Dacey.

She walked onto the elevator. Obviously, Dacey had had no sexual relationship with Cap, despite her Yellow Brick Road fantasies all these years that Cap might have gone AWOL and was living happily ever after with him.

Dacey just didn't figure. Dacey couldn't possibly be involved in this, she thought as the elevator wheezed to a halt at the fourth floor, because, as Doc had pointed out, Dacey had never even met Allan Gerlock.

Dacey had never even met Allan Gerlock.

Cap. Dacey . . .

The elevator door opened; she took one hurried step toward the room and the telephone and then she saw him. She froze, then lunged backward, her hand reaching to the opening in her jacket.

"Stop. Right there, Kate."

The blue eyes were the same as when she had first seen him in Vietnam—watchful, hard, alligator-flat. This no-longer-youthful man, the .357 in his hand held almost casually, was still a perfectly efficient killing machine, and once again she stared at him with admiration and dread.

Stuffing his gun hand in the pocket of his denim jacket, he said, "Do just as I say, Kate. Get out of the elevator. Hands nowhere but at your sides. Do just as I say—I've got your girlfriend."

Aimee. "Where is she?"

"Walk," he said. "To the other elevator."

Like the tumblers falling into place in the combination of a safe, she understood. And the surge of grief from what she understood, mixed in with fear, made her knees almost collapse.

The missing piece—of course—lay not among those who had met Allan Gerlock, but in the man who supposedly had not.

Dacey followed her onto the other elevator, pushing the button for the parking lot.

"Dacey, I need you to tell me where—"

"She's okay. Turn around, Kate, hands high on the wall."

Humiliation joined with fear. She would be a dead cop who had allowed herself to be disarmed. But her choices were simple: obey, or die now. She needed to know Aimee's whereabouts, she had to know whether Dacey had harmed Aimee because she had been in his path to his real target. Feeling the snout of a gun pressed into her spine, Kate could see in the elevator's mirrored wall Dacey reaching around her, inside her windbreaker, to extract the .38 from its holster.

"Not much firepower," he commented, stuffing the gun in an inside pocket of his jacket.

"Never needed much," she managed to say, and was amazed at the lack of quiver in her voice.

"You're a cool customer, I'll give you that," he said.

She did not answer. Could not. She was grateful to be braced against a wall; her knees were so weak, her legs so tremulous that she did not know if they would carry her. Aimee . . . Had he done anything to Aimee?

The elevator opened to a deserted rear lobby. "Out," Dacey said. Hands raised, she obeyed.

"Hands down," he ordered.

In the gray drizzle of the parking lot, guests took no notice of her and Dacey as they hurriedly loaded luggage into vehicles, including John Stafford who climbed into his Jeep Cherokee and drove off.

"Out to the street," Dacey said, moving up beside her, gun hand in his pocket. "Don't do anything dumb."

His voice and manner were assured, his walk confident. But then he had superb training and considerable war experience to draw on. She had one chance and one chance only: to break that confidence and concentration, to distract him. But her thought process seemed numb, her mind trapped in a spinning circle of anxiety over Aimee.

She did know that she would have a better chance in a car, whether she was driving or riding. "Walk," she said. "I thought a successful businessman like you would be driving a big car."

"I got a nice New Yorker parked a mile or so away. I don't want any traces of you in it. Just walk."

Emerging onto 17th Street she saw the same empty squad car she had observed from her room, not a cop in sight. Damn Carver and Duffy for taking her at her word about surveillance. Even if someone happened to be looking out a window of the Inn, she was not visible on this side of the street—and why would anyone make anything out of what appeared to be a casual stroll with Dacey?

She stopped and stared into his shark-cold eyes. "I need to know right now about Aimee."

"I haven't done anything to her."

"Where is she?"

"How should I know?"

"You told me—"

"I said what I said just to get you out of the hotel. Now move."

A well-dressed African-American woman herding two equally well-dressed little girls under a large umbrella came by, probably on their way to church, and Kate moved past them. Unconvinced by any of his answers, she said, "Tell me why you're doing this."

"Being cute, are you? A moron could see what was going on in that room last night. You're a cop all the way, you aren't about to let this go. Enough came out

from everybody that you'd put it together, figure it out
sometime—if not this weekend, sometime. When that
elevator door opened, one look at your face and I
could tell you already knew at least part of it."

She attempted a bluff. "I appreciate your confidence
in my detecting brilliance, Dacey, but I don't know
what you're talking about. I don't know anything except what you're—"

"Cut the bullshit. I caught a real break that I can
take care of this now. I get you out of the way I'm
home free."

She looked into his bearded face, then quickly away
from the glitter in his blue eyes. "Dacey—"

"I'm alibied, Kate. Every cop in the place left, so I
checked out too, at six this morning—left messages
where I'd be, did the whole nine yards." The words
were delivered with the machine-gun staccato of someone manic. "Easy getting back in, Kate, all it took was
a little tape and the desk clerk taking a leak."

She could well imagine. Tape over the lock on his
hotel door, tape over the third floor door to the stairway—just as he had done to swiftly escape after firing
the shots into her door. Tape over the door out to the
lobby. Check out, wait in the predawn gloom for the
well-illuminated desk clerk to leave his post, come back
into the hotel and up the lobby stairs to the third floor
and back into his room. The cop in the lobby must
have come on duty at seven or eight o'clock. While she
had been focused on the room doors on her own
fourth floor as she went out of the suite, undoubtedly
Dacey had been watching for her from the doorway to

the stairs. Compared to the jungles of Vietnam, the Inn on Liberty Square was a playground.

"Turn here," he said.

Preceding him around the corner, she looked up at the street sign: Church Street.

"I was looking to take you out the first time you came out of your room this morning," he said, as if he had been reading her thoughts. "But you're too smart, you went down that hallway like a commando. So I figured I'd get you coming back."

Kate waited, but when he did not continue she said, "Did you do anything to my partner?"

"Your partner," he repeated contemptuously. "Maybe yes, maybe no."

With effort, she played along with his cruel game. "What difference will it make if you tell me?"

He chuckled. "It could make a difference."

Wanting to pummel the truth from him, Kate probed cautiously, "How do you know somebody else didn't see you in the hotel?"

"I'm checked out, gone. They'll just be wrong," Dacey said assuredly.

"I suppose that's true," Kate said, regretting her question. If Dacey had not done anything to anyone else, especially Aimee, she did not want him thinking he should go back and tidy up. This man was zeroed in like a crack addict; he was in a homicidal zone that would imperil anyone in his way.

Dacey said, "Then it was just a matter of getting the drop on you."

"You got the drop on me all right," Kate said, and the terror she had been holding at bay leaped and engulfed her. No danger she had ever faced in her life or her work had prepared her to face the immediate certainty of her death.

She glanced around her at the buildings, at passersby, seeking any hope, any sort of possibility. But she and Dacey looked innocuous, a man and woman of similar age out strolling on a drizzly Sunday morning, and the passersby were mostly parents, their attention given to protecting children in their neatly pressed Sunday best from the elements. The stylish brick buildings she passed displayed only their stony Victorian facades to her.

"I tried to let you go," Dacey said. "You get yourself and your girlfriend out of town, none of this happens."

"Don't blame me for that man's death, Dacey," she said harshly. "I'm not the one who killed him. And I still don't understand why anybody had to die."

"Things just got outta hand." He spoke almost apologetically. "I didn't intend for any of this to happen, Kate—I mean it. We didn't have an idea in the world about killing anybody."

We? "What happened?"

But she already knew some of it. Cap was dead. Had been dead all these long twenty-five years. Cap had never reached the DMZ. Because Dacey—and someone else, apparently—had killed him first. But *why?*

"In here," Dacey said.

Taking her arm with the hand not holding the gun, he turned her into a small parklike area just off Church Street. So this was where it would happen, she thought, her boots soundlessly crushing wet, dark gold leaves. In this strange city, in the rain, in a place thick with trees and filled with the autumn colors of her childhood . . .

Dacey said, "Cap was supposed to be on a chopper going up to the Third Division at Khe Sanh—that's all he was told."

She remembered her leave-taking of Cap, the brave, nonchalant faces they had put on for each other. After all, they were still in the same country, weren't they? She had hugged him good-bye, and he had promised to be careful . . .

"Will Maloney was going up there with medical supplies. So he took Cap. And I took him to the chopper and went along for the ride. Will and me, we had something to settle with Cap."

She tensed, not wanting to hear what was coming.

"Sit," he said, gesturing to a park bench, its surface beaded with moisture.

Unzipping his jacket, he leaned back against the broad trunk of an oak tree facing her, and took his gun hand from his pocket, holding the barrel angled downward, concealed just inside his jacket. She smelled the moldering damp of leaves and earth, could feel wetness from the bench, an icy chill soaking into the back of her jeans.

"Will and me, we had serious beefs with this guy." His sensual lips were turned down, his tone aggrieved. "I mean, I called in napalm on villages over there, on women and kids, and this cherry lieutenant doesn't have a single fucking clue. He goes out in the countryside and helps the fucking gooks, the *enemy*, for chrissakes, and he thinks he's a hero. He can't see how they're laughing their heads off when he turns his back, how they're tossing grenades and anything else they got down our throats. Then this dumbshit cherry lieutenant turns us in for taking target practice on a fucking water buffalo.''

Slouching against the tree, he crossed his ankles. "His leaving was payback time. So Will lands the chopper on the beach and we explain a few things, and he smarts off and we knock him around some. And knowing Cap's queer and all, we . . . have a little fun with him. Then Will takes off over the China Sea and dumps him.'' He shook his head. "I didn't know Will was gonna do it, I swear.''

Of course you didn't, she thought in intensifying rage. "Sure," she said gratingly. "You and Will assault a superior officer and expect to just walk away.''

"Look, Kate, here I am on my way home, I'm outta there free and clear, I don't need any shit. Okay, I was on a little meth, we wanted to rough him up a little, that was all, for what he did to us. It just got outta hand.''

She said, her eyes fixed on his expensive cowboy boots, "And then the two of you realized people knew Cap was on that chopper.''

"You got it.''

"So you take Cap's insignia, his dog tags, you go on up to Khe Sanh.'' She would not look up at him, knowing her contempt, her loathing for him would be written so clearly on her face that she might silence him, propel him into action. Cap's murder had to have been premeditated. This cold-blooded killer had figured it all out beforehand, had removed the items

from Cap's body before he—and the "he" had to be
Dacey, not Will—had tossed him, whether dead or
alive, into the South China Sea. Rage coursed through
her, obliterating even fear.

Dacey said, "We had to cover ourselves. Nothing
looked easier—pretend to be him, be a cherry lieutenant for a day and then disappear. Will comes back the
next day and picks me up—simple. The one thing I
don't expect on God's green earth is this Allan dude
who's waiting for him to turn up."

"So you spent an entire evening with Allan pretending to be Cap."

"Had no choice."

And that was the entire answer to why Allan Gerlock
had to die—he knew Dacey as Cap Pearson.

"I don't understand," she said.

"I thought it would be easy. I thought Gerlock knew
as little about Cap as I did about Gerlock. So we have
drinks in his quarters and all of a sudden this guy
comes on to me—and I mean hard, and I haul off and
deck him."

She was beginning to understand.

"So he's all confused and scared witless and telling
me he'd never do anything like that except he heard
I was for sure gay."

"I see," she murmured.

"I told him to forget it, there was no problem, and
to this day there'd never have been a problem except
the two of you decide to turn up here together, and
Melanie tells me you're out of the closet now. So you
and Gerlock are gonna talk, I know you're gonna compare notes about this. Once you find out he came on

to me and I decked him, you'd know the guy he met wasn't Cap." He shrugged, then added, "I did my best, I tried to save you both."

Choking on her fury, she could not bring herself to answer this plea for understanding.

"I could've killed you two days ago, easy. I've had to kill women, I'm not real fond of it. But you know how easy it is to kill somebody, Kate?"

"No, I don't," she said with unconcealed scorn.

"You wouldn't," he said. "You may be a cop but you're a pussy, like all females. The first time, it's the most gut-wrenching thing that's ever happened in your whole fucking life. The second time it's the pits too. After that—it's nothing. It gets comfortable. Real comfortable."

Out of the corner of her eye she saw him lift the gun, point it at her as if in demonstration. "They train us to kill people every which way to Sunday. But they don't train you how to come back to the World. No laws over there in Nam, then you come back, they just throw you back where you don't fit anymore and they say, obey all the rules. People in this country, they got no idea the time bombs walking around their streets. People, they got no fucking idea . . ."

Remembering the psychological profiles of the serial killers she had been looking at over the past days, she asked numbly, "Have you killed other people since you've been back?"

He turned over his wrist to look at his watch, as if to gauge how much more time he could safely allocate to this conversation. "Put it this way, I don't take any shit from anybody. But Cap did me one hell of a big

favor as it turned out. Didn't you wonder how a nobody like me could get himself all those cleaning fran-
chises?"

"No, I assumed you'd earned your success."

"Fucking goddamn right I did. All I needed was just
one break. Golden boys like Cap Pearson, they get all
the breaks."

She stared grimly at the leaf-strewn, soggy earth. It
was a waste of breath to point out that Cap Pearson
was a self-made man who had had no more breaks—
and actually far fewer—than Dacey.

Dacey said, "Here I am back in the World with this
guy's dog tags and all his ID, he's got no close relatives.
So who would you rather be? An ex-Marine lieutenant
with a college degree, or an ex-Marine convicted felon
with a family that thinks he's dog shit? So I use his ID
for a few years. But who'd ever think there'd be all this
shit over the MIAs? So I have to be me again—but by
then I have a few bucks to give me a boost. And you
know what, today it isn't so bad being me."

Kate could feel hate stacking up inside her like
bricks forming a wall.

He stirred, uncrossed his feet, and she knew she had
only moments left. If he put a bullet in her, she had
few options. But she had every expectation from his
previous MO, and from the fact that people were all
around, that he would again hold a gun to her back
while he cut her throat, down to her vocal cords.

She got up from the bench. She would not go like
some meek little lamb. She would use what little advantage she could gain from his using a knife to do at
least as well as Allan Gerlock had. She would fight, rake

her fingernails down any piece of his skin she could reach; she would leave a souvenir under her fingernails that would match up with his DNA, and her police family would damn well find him.

"You aren't worth wearing a rat's dog tags let alone Cap Pearson's," she snarled.

"And you don't have the rat's chance you think you do," he said, smiling.

As he took a step toward her, she tensed her entire body, drew up her fingers in a taut arch, willing her nails to become lethal cat's claws.

And released an involuntary gasp of amazement.

Dacey jerked to a halt in midstride, almost looked behind him. Then said derisively, "The old pretend-you-see-something-behind-him tr—"

Two arms savagely grappled Dacey below the elbows and yanked his gun down, propelled him forward.

The .357 went off with a *BLAM*, and Dacey howled from shock and from the bullet that exploded the top of one expensive boot into bloody shards before he was driven face-forward into the mud at Kate's feet.

Blue-clad figures, guns drawn, swarmed all around Kate; she saw Rudy Doyle kick Dacey's gun away.

Jill Manners slammed a knee into Dacey's back, wrenching one of his arms up behind him and snapping on a handcuff. "Asshole, you might figure a light-footed little pussy like me could come over wet leaves without making a sound," she snarled. Ignoring Dacey's yowls of pain, Jill wrenched his other arm around and snicked on the matching handcuff.

"Nice going, Kate," Carver said, strolling up to her from out of the crowd of uniformed police. Holstering

his weapon, straightening his tie, he said with his embalmed smile, "Until it looked like you were gonna
jump this turd all by yourself. You got a confession, I
trust?"

"Holy God," she whispered, her mind still trying to
catch up with this lightning series of events. "Aimee,"
she uttered. "What about Aimee?"

"Miss Grant's in your hotel room, she knows something's going down, she has an officer with her. We
guaranteed your safety."

Her knees gave way; the surge of relief combined
with spent adrenaline and the evaporation of her an-
ticipation of death had paralyzed her. She collapsed
onto the bench.

"Take it easy, just sit there," Duffy advised.

"Pretty smart move," Carver said, patting her on the
shoulder, "raising your hands as you left the elevator."

"Thanks," she managed. "So David Olson saw me?"

"Yeah, he's a good man. But we had our sights on
you. Jacobs in the lobby pretending to read the paper,
plainclothes guys in the street and the parking lot. We
had to get the drop on turd-face here or set up a sniper
so you and the civilians wouldn't get hurt. Him standing against a tree nearly screwed us. So Jill here did
her act."

As Jill, with seeming reluctance, got up from Dacey,
Rudy Doyle grabbed the connecting link of the hand-
cuffs and yanked Dacey to his feet, to another howl of
pain.

Kate was beginning to think she liked Rudy Doyle.

"Christ," Dacey muttered, his face greenish.

Patting Dacey down, Jill removed the .38 from within

his jacket, looked at it more closely, tucked it inside her own jacket. Kate knew that the gun would be returned to her under less public circumstances.

"Take him, read him his rights," Carver said. Inspecting Dacey's foot, he added, "Get him in the ambulance."

"Yeah, we're real sorry about your pain," Duffy said to Dacey.

Kate took one final look at him. His eyes, containing agony and a dawning of fear, met hers. Wanting to attack and batter him, she instead said, "It takes a real genius to shoot himself in the foot." And from all around her came the gratifying sound of cops mocking Dacey with their raucous laughter.

Carver said, "We got word this morning, Kate. You were absolutely right. The great state of Kentucky faxed a copy of an auto license taken out in 1970 under the name of Charles A. Pearson, and wouldn't you know Dacey's mug is on it."

Grinning, Jill reached both hands out to Kate, pulled her firmly to her feet.

My police family, Kate thought. Even in this awful city.

16

"**K**ATE, thank God you called. This case—uh, I know you're up to your eyeballs there, how are things going?"

"Torrie, everything's under control," Kate assured her. "They just made an arrest. I'll tell you all about it when I get home." Sitting at the table in the suite, her feet up on the seat of an adjacent chair, the phone at her ear, she felt an infinite indebtedness to Torrie for this refocus of her mind and emotions, however temporary. "So what's going on?"

"I did just like you said, concentrated on being professional. Once we took statements, things didn't add up. Leila Alcott—that's the young nurse who started this investigation—her story of when she claims this all happened doesn't corroborate with the doctor's scheduled rounds or with anybody's schedule except hers."

"I see," Kate said.

"Yes, I began to, too. So I took her into the station yesterday, we talked for a long time."

"On tape?" Kate gazed at the gray sky outside the window.

"I thought some informal and sympathetic listening would work better with Leila."

"I see. And that's fine." Regardless of the sincerity of Torrie's approach or her motivation, it was good police procedure, damn good detective work. But she knew better than to suggest any other motive to Torrie.

"She has no memory of anything she did. She was hoping against hope we'd find out it positively wasn't her."

"So whatever happened to this boy, if anything did, it may be accidental, not intentional."

"That's still hard to say, Kate. We'll know more after the post on Monday."

She liked the objectivity from this new detective. "Listen, Torrie, all good pathologists want an exchange of information. They want detectives to tell them things about a crime scene, it helps with interpretation. Carruthers will be doing the post—she autopsies the children, and she's good. Make sure you give her chapter and verse on exactly the circumstances of this situation."

Eyes fixed on the grayness filling the window, she was remembering Horatio, and Bernie and Rachel's attempts to save him. And Doc: *"We were no more morally right in saving that boy's life than his Vietnamese family was morally wrong to abandon him."*

Had Horatio's Vietnamese family acted with any less morality than America's save-life-at-all-cost medical profession?

"Torrie, is the press involved?"

"A *Times* reporter asked some questions, but there's been no follow-up."

With any luck, there wouldn't be. This was the kind

of case which press attention could provide with an unnatural life of its own.

"Make sure you give the full and complete particulars to the district attorney's office." In a case where people of conscience were involved, and where the outcome from a legal standpoint would be a suspended sentence at most ... "Give everyone the chance to have common sense prevail, Torrie."

"I hear you."

She could not imagine that anyone would want to have anything to do with this case. "I have a feeling this one will end up a DA reject."

"Yeah, but that won't end it, Kate. Leila Alcott is in a real crisis over this. But I think I'm making some inroads into helping her with it."

Kate suddenly needed to be off this phone. The reunion with Aimee only minutes ago was not enough; she urgently needed to be with her again. And to be with her Vietnam family.

"Let me tell you something, Torrie. I suspect some sort of destiny put me in Washington, D.C. this week so the perfect detective could handle this case."

"Kate—thank you for that. Thank you."

Leaning on the restaurant table with her arms crossed in front of her, Melanie said, "I guess I'm just plain dumb. What good does it do if Dacey gets you out of town, Kate? At the reunion Allan is still going to know him as Cap."

"If Katie leaves, Dacey leaves," Bernie said. "He doesn't turn up at the reunion either."

Nodding, Woody added, "If Allan comes to the reunion and Kate and Dacey aren't here, nobody's the wiser if he thinks Dacey is Cap. He thinks Cap's an MIA just like the rest of us."

"Exactly right," Kate said.

"Wait a minute," Melanie said. "If Dacey just doesn't show up and lets Allan meet Kate—exactly what happens?"

Kate said, nodding at her, "Exactly what Dacey knows will happen. Allan and I connect on our common ground—being gay people in Vietnam—and we talk about Cap. I ask Allan to tell me about Cap and the day he disappeared—"

Melanie interjected, "And that's when Allan tells you about coming on to Cap and Cap punching him."

"Right," Kate said. "And that's when I realize the man Allan met couldn't possibly have been Cap."

Doc said, "What an irony—the big clue turns out to be that Dacey's the only one of us Allan never met."

"Or so we all assumed," Kate said. "It's the clue I almost missed. I thought it cleared him. Till I put it together with the fact that this was Allan's and my first reunion—and Dacey's."

"Wait a minute," Martin objected, grinning, "it was mine and Gabe's and Rachel's too."

"Gee, so did they get the right guy?" Melanie asked disingenuously.

Kate's laughter was more boisterous than anyone else's. Every nerve cell in her body felt energized, she was soaring on an exuberance of relief, of deliverance.

All of the group—Martin, Doc and his wife, Bernie and Ralph, Melanie, Rachel, Gabe, and Woody—had gathered around a big table in the Patriot Room to

share three bottles of Moet champagne, compliments
of Martin, and served personally and with great cere-
mony by David Olson, who looked as relieved and
buoyant as Kate felt. Aimee sat with an arm around
Kate, which she sometimes tightened but would not
remove, despite Kate's earlier semi-truthful protesta-
tion: "I was never in real danger."

"I don't care," Aimee had declared. "I don't care
what anybody here thinks about us. We're getting out
of this town and never coming back."

"It won't be that simple," Kate had said. "I'm now
a major witness—"

"I don't want to hear about it. I'm sick of being
scared out of my wits, I'm sick of you having more guts
than sense."

If Aimee only knew about my true gut level, the full
dimension of my fear, Kate thought. She had not mentioned being virtually immobilized by terror that Aimee had become Dacey's next victim. But she hardly
minded Aimee's embrace; its warmth and possessive-
ness were a restorative.

Aimee said to her now, "So this is why Dacey kept
in touch with you all these years."

"Sure," Gabe said. "If you and Allan ever showed
up together at one of these things, he had to know it."

"And here all the time I thought he was crazy about
me," Kate joked. Again there was laughter all around;
her own hilarity verged on an uncontrollable laughing
jag.

"What a reunion," Bernie said. "We've been under
fire here like we were in Vietnam. Or at least some of
us."

"Dacey," Melanie hissed. "The fucking evil bastard."

"May his nuts roast in hell," Bernie said. She clutched a glass of champagne in one hand, Ralph's arm in the other. She looked, Kate thought, pale and sick. Bernie obviously needed to do something about her drinking, but Kate knew she was hardly the one to say much. She would ask Rachel to talk to her.

"Allan was one heck of a good guy," Woody said, shaking his head.

"I thought I was pretty close to Allan," Rachel said somberly, "but I didn't have a clue he was gay."

"I don't think any of us did," Gabe said, and there were murmurs of agreement from around the table.

Melanie said, "All I know is, he decided he was coming to this reunion when I told him about Kate and Aimee. I think he was ready to tell us the truth about—"

Woody slammed his glass on the table. "Allan tells any one of us about this years ago, we put it all together, Dacey's ass gets nailed, none of this happens—"

"He couldn't, Woody," Doc said, staring at him. "Now could he?"

Woody met Doc's stare. "Yeah. I guess maybe he couldn't."

"Don't ask, don't tell," Aimee muttered.

"The what-ifs can go on forever," Kate said evenly. "The fact is, Dacey chose to kill Cap. And Allan."

In the silence she said, "I need to get down to the Municipal Center." She would leave all of them now, to their own further postmortem.

Only her status with these D.C. cops—"Come down to our cop shop whenever you're ready," Carver had told her—had allowed her to ameliorate some of her chaotic emotion in the comfort of Aimee and these friends before giving her official statement of the morning's events.

"To us," Martin said, raising his glass.

"To us," Kate repeated solemnly, looking into Aimee's eyes as she spoke the words.

As soon as she could, she would try to find a way to tell Aimee of her newfound sense of wholeness—and to assure Aimee that she must waste no guilt over events that had nothing to do with her. Allan Gerlock's death this weekend had been as inexorable and unpreventable as a Greek tragedy; it had been set into motion fully twenty-five years ago; it was all a part of the age-darkened shadow of Vietnam.

Kate gazed at each face around the table knowing that she would never see most of them again. War had thrown them all together and under its stresses they had bonded as comrades. War was what they held in common then—and all they held in common now. What could she could possibly add to Martin's present-day life, or to Doc's? There was nothing she could add to Gabe, or to Woody. Or to Melanie. Or to Rachel . . . not even to Rachel. Bernie, yes—Bernie, Kate sensed that somehow, in some degree, Bernie would continue in her life. But as for the rest of the group, the simple truth was, there was no need for any further continuity—for the simple reason that the connection among all of them could never be broken.

Cards at Christmas. Until an inner core urgency

drew some of them together again in a future reunion so that they might once more band together as comrades, eyewitnesses to one another's presence in a foreign land during a year that had indelibly marked all of them and rerouted all their lives.

For her, the essential lesson of this weekend lay in the difference between who she had been before she came here, and who she was now. She had restored the part of herself that she had tried to cut off. Unsparingly taken in her year in Vietnam and integrated it with her self. For that greater wholeness she had Aimee to thank. Aimee needed to know it, understand it. . . .

After more clinks of glasses all around to a toast that Kate, absent with her thoughts, did not hear, Doc said, "To the Vietnam class of sixty-eight and sixty-nine."

More clinks, then Rachel said somberly, "There's still one thing left to do. We all need to say good-bye to Cap."

Bernie said, "How about we all go there when Kate gets back."

No need to ask where, Kate thought as murmurs of assent and nods came from around the table.

Aimee leaned into her and asked quietly, "Can you handle this?"

Kate clasped her hand. "It's time."

17

IN the shadows of evening the gathering separated into two units: Kate and Aimee, Bernie, Rachel, Melanie—and Jill Manners, invited to the Inn for dinner by Kate, and included for this occasion by consensus. In their own group outside the entrance to Arlington National Cemetery, Woody, Gabe, Martin, and Doc walked together, quietly talking. Doc wore plain green military fatigues and a cap with a circular patch that read: THE FEW. THE PROUD. THE MARINES.

As a breezy mist laid beads of moisture on jackets and windbreakers, Aimee came to a halt with the rest of the women and gazed up at the six great spotlighted bronze figures straining to plant the American flag on Iwo Jima during World War II.

"The only good war, they say," Kate mused, contemplating the dramatically shadowed giant sculpture. "Sixty thousand Marines landed, twenty-three thousand of us killed or wounded. The Japanese fought to the death—only a thousand left alive when we finally took the island."

Trying to comprehend such carnage, Aimee read the gold lettering inscribed within a wreath carved on the granite base: UNCOMMON VALOR WAS A COMMON VIRTUE.

"Fifty-eight Marines in the entire history of the Corps received the Medal of Honor," Kate said. "Five of them helped raise that flag. Three of the five were killed in action."

"I never realized how much you knew about the Corps," Aimee said. "You're proud you served in the Marines."

"I am," Kate said, hands in her jacket pockets, her eyes focused on the stars and stripes blowing in the cloud-swept night. "Our oldest and finest fighting unit . . . I've always been proud I served in the Corps."

"I'm proud of you. I'm proud that you served," Aimee said.

"Navy nurses were on Iwo too, Katie," Bernie said quietly from beside her. "We came in under fire and got the wounded out."

"I know you did, Bernie."

"We were in all the wars, good or bad," Rachel added.

Martin, Gabe, Woody, and Doc had heard some of this conversation; Martin slid one arm around Bernie, the other around Rachel. "Patriotic . . . courageous," he said gently. "The young men and women in all our wars have been our very best."

"Even in Nam," Gabe said.

As the group approached the Vietnam Women's Memorial, the men again split away as if at some unspoken signal.

Ever since the meeting and the toasts in the Patriot Room, Kate felt as if she were walking along a path remarkable for its absolute rightness, had felt it in everything she had done this day in this city, felt it even more strongly now.

Liberation underlay all the events of this day. Confirmation of Cap's death had released her to reclaim her true memory, her true pride in this city of wide, tree-lined streets, of brick and marble structures of richness and grandeur, of ancient gray-stoned churches and multitudes of heroic statuary. She walked now within sight of the sublime monument dedicated to the leader whose profoundly grieving face held full knowledge of a nation torn apart by war. She walked within sight of the thirteen pillars holding up the golden Capitol dome, and the Statue of Freedom.

"I was here when they dedicated our memorial a year ago this month," Bernie said to her now as they reached the Vietnam Women's Memorial. "It was . . ." Bernie did not finish.

Walking slowly around the bronze sculpture of three nurses and a soldier, Kate looked into the faces of the nurses forever frozen in their compassion, anxiety, fatigue. The wounded soldier, a bandage covering his forehead and eyes, held in the arms of the nurse providing him life support, his concealing bandage signifying the anonymity of virtually all the soldiers whose lives the nurses had fought for . . .

"That soldier will make it, you can tell," Melanie said.

"He will," Bernie agreed. She gestured to the standing figure, a nurse looking anxiously off in the distance with a hand on the arm of the nurse holding the soldier. "This one here could be me. Waiting for a dustoff to come in."

"Or asking God why all this is happening," Rachel said. "For me, she says it all." And she nodded toward a kneeling nurse looking at an empty helmet in despair, frustration, helplessness, horror.

Kate glanced around to locate Aimee; she was walking with Jill, both women talking softly and engrossed in the sculpture.

Rachel took Kate's hand. "Ready, Kate?"

"Yes," Kate said.

Linking her other hand with Bernie, Rachel moved off; Bernie took Melanie's hand.

"Aimee," Kate called to her, but Aimee held back.

"You belong with them," she said.

"I'm an intruder here," Jill murmured to Aimee.

"No more so than me," Aimee answered.

"I know this is very, very special to all of you."

"Kate and the others want you here," Aimee said simply. "They've honored us both by including us." No one else from the reunion group had accompanied this core group—Doc's wife and Bernie's husband were back at the Inn.

Jill, a white windbreaker tied around her shoulders, inclined her head toward Kate. "How she handled herself this morning—you should have been there."

Aimee replied with a nod. No way on earth would she have wanted to witness Kate in peril of her life.

Jill said quietly, "When I was a kid there was this TV ad with a black woman in an Army uniform in a really technical job telling me, Be all that you can be. I grew up wanting to be just like her. My cousin Jamille—she's the one. A Gulf War veteran, in training now as a fighter pilot. She says the Vietnam women made the big breakthrough, made it all possible . . ." Jill said, pointing to Kate, "*That's* the woman I really wanted to be when I grew up."

Aimee was focused on Kate, who walked a dozen paces in front of her holding hands with Rachel and Bernie and Melanie; they had reached an outer perimeter lined with illuminated, glass-covered cases protecting the directories listing the names of all those killed or missing in action, and the location of those names on the Vietnam Memorial. Woody, Aimee saw, had gone over to one of the lighted cases.

If you could somehow manage to not look up and take in the whole of what you know is coming because you've read about it, seen the pictures . . .

She was composing in her head—the refuge she always fled into when she must try to grasp the inconceivable. Disassociation, disconnection. Composing a letter to someone who would judge her on her objectivity, on her impartiality. . . .

The way to do this has to be one step at a time. Enter this place, and look only at the first shiny black panel, it has one line and five names etched into it. . . . Then to the next shiny black panel, same width, wedged deeper into the earth, three lines of five names. The next one, deeper still, more lines of five names. You're descending into the earth. . . . The height of the shiny black panels waist level, many more lines and many names now on the shiny black panels, and the lines and names are shoulder level and you go down and down into the earth, each shiny black panel with its lines and lines of five names illuminated by a small spotlight imbedded in the brick and granite pathway, and the shiny black panels are head-high and they hold more names on more and more lines, and you're absorbed into a universe of names, the shiny black Wall high above your head and all those panels and all those lines are uttering their names at you . . . And you are in an open grave with all those names.

Eyes closed, shuddering with her tears, Jill's arm around her, Aimee wiped her face. And again looked.

All around you are people like you, every age and color, their stunned faces surely mirrors of yours. They weep as you weep because, no matter what they expected, the stark meaning of this place has swallowed them whole as it has devoured you, and they lean and touch the Wall dazed by this unimaginable accounting of loss, just as you do. They touch a fingertip because they have to feel the carving on just one of the gold-lettered names just as you do. They look at the American flags, the state flags, the gay pride flags, the flowers, the folded notes and letters, the photos, the crosses . . . all the tributes that lean against the panels all along both long, long sides of this Wall of remembrance.

In a tidal wave of grief, Kate watched Melanie kneel down to touch a blossom in a bouquet of carnations tied with red, white, and blue ribbons.

Melanie said, "Those boys in the field, I remember to this day how they smelled, to this day I smell them in my dreams . . ."

"They did smell, Melanie," Bernie said wonderingly, the fingers of one hand caressing a name on the Wall, "they'd come in and there was that smell . . ."

"Earth . . . sweat . . . fear . . . all mixed together," Rachel said softly, her reflection caught in the shiny black granite of the Wall.

"In Nam they called the boys in the field kings," Melanie said, brushing the fingertips of both hands along the Wall. "I walked with kings. I served with kings."

Doc, trembling, stood looking at the names, Martin's arm around him. "A list of our failures. I failed them. Any one of them could have been my patient, it's a list of failures . . ."

"You saved lives, Doc, you were a healer," Kate uttered, almost bereft of voice.

"We lost so many," Martin said. "The ones I lost—I don't even know their names . . ."

"What good did any of this do?" Doc asked. "What did we accomplish? What was the meaning of all this obscene sacrifice?"

Kate whispered, "I've been thinking about this for twenty-five years—"

Woody said gently, "Kate, over here. . . ."

The group followed Woody and Kate. Woody was pointing, but Kate reached up, sensing where the name was before she read the letters, CHARLES A. PEARSON. First she touched the tiny cross after his name, the cross signifying missing in action; it would be changed now to a diamond. Then she traced the letters. She felt fingers touch hers: Rachel's. Bernie's hand on top of Rachel's. Melanie's hand. Doc. Woody. Gabe. Martin. All their hands touching hers, touching Cap.

"It was so meaningless," Doc sobbed.

Kate said, "After twenty-five years I think maybe its great value is that we understand that."

Watching all of them with their hands together on

the Wall, Aimee thought of the Iwo Jima Memorial, and froze them in tableau in her mind, knowing she would remember this forever.

In the absolute rightness of this day, Kate thought, it was appropriate that it had rained this entire weekend and that it rained harder now. Grateful for the rightness of the rain in this place, Kate lifted her face to the rain, let it join with the tears down her face.

AFTERWORD

Out of the considerable research that underpins this novel—books, magazine and newspaper articles, films—my profound appreciation is owed to several essential sources. First, and most of all, to the unforgettable, moving, inspirational *A Piece of My Heart: The Stories of 26 American Women Who Served in Vietnam* by Keith Walker: Presidio Press, Novato, CA. Also to *Vietnam: The Other War* by Charles Anderson: Warner Books, New York, NY; to Tim Page's *Nam*: Alfred Knopf, New York, NY; *Serving in Silence* by Margarethe Cammermeyer with Chris Fisher: Viking, New York, NY; *Nurses in Vietnam: The Forgotten Veterans*, Editor Dan Freedman, Associate Editor, Jacqueline Rhoads: Texas Monthly Press, Austin, TX; *Lesbians in the Military Speak Out* by Winni S. Weber: Madwoman Press, Northboro, MA; *Conduct Unbecoming: Gays and Lesbians in the U.S. Military* by Randy Shilts: St. Martin's Press, New York, NY; *Celebration of the Vietnam Women's Memorial November 10–12, 1993*: Vietnam Women's Memorial Project, Washington, D.C.; *Strange Ground: Americans in Vietnam 1945–1975: An Oral History* by Harry Maurer: Henry Holt and Company, New York, NY; *U.S. Marines in Vietnam: High Mobility and Standdown 1969* by Charles R. Smith: History and Museums Division, Headquarters, U.S. Marine Corps, Washington, D.C.